I0534034

WOLF DISTRESSED

ENSNARED BY THE PACK: BOOK 4

TESSA COLE

Gryphon's Gate Publishing

Wolf Distressed

Copyright © 2022 Tessa Cole

All rights reserved. No part of this book may be reproduced in any form or by any means without written consent, excepting brief quotes used in reviews.

This is a work of fiction. Names, places, characters, and events are entirely the product of the author's imagination or are used fictitiously, and any resemblance to persons, living or dead, actual locals, events, or organizations is coincidental.

Gryphon's Gate Publishing

550 King St. N.

PO Box 42088 Conestoga

Waterloo, ON

N2L 6K5

Print ISBN: 978-1-990587-20-7

KNOX

AUDREY!

I woke with a start, shifting into my wolf form before I was fully conscious. I'd passed out after my mate had saved me from my furious wolf and, just like the last time my wolf had taken over, my brothers had left me in the private sacred grove behind the Residence to recover.

Except this time, instead of waking groggy and exhausted, a burning urgency screamed through my veins.

Audrey was in trouble and I had to get to her. Her emotions roaring inside me were stronger than Bishop's when he was upset, but I didn't know how that was possible.

A mating bond didn't connect two people like my twin bond connected me and Bishop. Mates were more attuned to their partners, but not to the extent that they felt each other's emotions like they were their own.

Surely, I would have noticed something before now, especially during that moment when she'd yelled at me for hurting her. She'd been conscious for five days, angry with me, and almost drowned, and I hadn't noticed more than a hint of emotions that weren't mine or Bishop's. The emotions couldn't be hers...

Except I knew in every fiber of my being that the panic and pain coursing through me was Audrey's.

It didn't matter if it made sense or not, I had to go to her.

She was the piece of my soul that I hadn't realized was missing until I'd thought she was going to drown in that flash flood. Even if we hadn't been bonded and her death wouldn't have affected me like it did now, I'd go after her.

She was mine. My fate. My mate. My responsibility to protect.

My wolf had known the truth the moment he'd caught her scent, and he was still furious that I'd denied him for so long. And while I didn't know exactly what had happened in the arena, I knew he'd have completely taken over if she hadn't begged him to release me.

I didn't deserve her kindness. She'd have survived fine if my wolf had completely taken over, probably lived a better life than the one she was facing now. He'd never hurt her, not like I had, and surely would in the future.

I had to make it up to her, had to figure out how to be a good mate. Except I wouldn't be able to do that if she died, and I feared, from the emotions coursing through me, that that was about to happen.

I didn't know why I believed that. I could only feel her fear and heartache. But something about that fear, how it ran so cold and deep, cutting into my soul, told me she was in immediate danger.

Bishop, I said, reaching out to him mentally as I bounded out of the grove and followed the pull on my soul, praying it would take me to Audrey.

Knox? His mental voice was groggy as if he was barely awake. Then he registered the urgency in my voice and I felt our connection strengthen. *What's wrong? How are you—? I—?*

A confusing muddle of emotions and half thoughts rushed through me but I couldn't understand why he was confused.

Of course, I also didn't remember anything after Cyrus and Bishop released the collar containing the wolf half of my soul and before I was staring down into Audrey's wide brown eyes with the knowledge that she'd asked my wolf to give me back to her. Anything could have happened. I didn't even know how long my wolf had possessed me.

And none of that mattered.

Audrey is in trouble.

A flash of panic snapped through our twin bond, now second in strength to my bond with Audrey, something I hadn't thought possible. *Where? How?*

I don't know, I growled back, frustrated that I couldn't answer those simple questions.

The pull on my soul compelled me through the Residence's gates and into Old Town, and my frustration grew stronger. *Why the hell isn't she in the Residence?*

She isn't—? Cyrus? Bishop asked, adding our older brother to our telepathic conversation. *Where's Audrey?*

I— He paused for too long and even though I didn't have an emotional connection with Cyrus like I did with Bishop, I knew something was up.

What did you do? I demanded, the pull taking me out of Old Town and drawing me north, following the outside edge of the towering Old Town wall.

Nova, Cyrus said, not answering my question. *Where's Audrey?*

She wasn't in her suite, the grove, or the gardens. I figured she didn't want to be found right now, Nova replied. *I told Finn to keep an eye out for her. She's probably exploring her new home and wants a little space.*

Why would she want space? Bishop asked, his worry growing.

You know— Nova began but I released my connection with them, not bothering to hear whatever excuse they were going to come up with. If they didn't know where she was, they couldn't help her.

Clearly, she was outside the Residence walls, and it looked like she was in the northern part of Stonehaven, a part that despite all our initiatives was still a seedy part of town. It was closest to the road connecting the town to the mountain pass and was near to the market and housed the warehouses and cheap inns and bars that poorer traveling merchants liked to visit. Foreigners weren't restricted to the area, but most of them stayed where the food and lodging wouldn't eat into their profits.

Finn, I barked, praying he was within reach of my telepathic ability.

I was a strong alpha so I could communicate with someone farther away from me than most shifters, but I still wasn't strong enough to talk to someone on the other side of town. Not even Cyrus could do that, and he'd worked to extend his ability beyond what anyone else in the pack could do.

Knox? Finn asked, surprise coloring his mental voice.

Yeah, I didn't usually communicate with the pack's betas except for Nova who was really more like a sister than a beta. Technically they were my betas as well, not just my brothers', but I never wanted the responsibility of being one of the pack's alphas. I was the person least suited to the job because I didn't want to talk to anyone.

Except if it saved Audrey, I'd talk to the whole damn pack and deal with the emotional fallout later.

Anything to protect her.

And the first guy who might know something was the beta in command of the town's watch.

Audrey, I said. I couldn't let his surprise pull him off topic and I needed to know where she was. Now. *Where's Audrey?*

Nova mentioned something, Finn replied. *Why—?*

Where is she? Do any of the watchmen have eyes on her? I

asked and a burst of alpha power escaped my control and blasted out around me.

The half dozen people on the street, some barely in sight at the far end, dropped to their knees in submission while Finn groaned, my power reaching through our telepathic connection.

Fuck, Knox, Cyrus snapped. *Pull your power back. You just dropped everyone in the kitchen.*

The kitchen? He was still in the kitchen? Why wasn't he looking for Audrey?

Fury roared through me and another blast of power broke through my control.

What the fuck are you still doing in the Residence? I demanded, not caring that my power slip was big enough that it reached all the way to the Residence. *You should be looking for her! Audrey's in trouble and she's somewhere in the north end of town.*

Where in the north end? Cyrus asked.

I don't know! I didn't know anything. I didn't know what kind of trouble she was in or if she was already hurt.

All I knew was that she needed me and I had to go to her.

Vida says she saw her near Jaxon's smithy about an hour ago, Finn said. *I'll send a team to bring her in.*

You're not arresting her, I snarled.

Sending a team would scare her. Even I could tell people in authority made her nervous, especially if it looked like she was going to be accused of something. Anyone who'd spent two seconds with her would know that, and I was furious that Finn automatically jumped to the conclusion that she'd done something wrong.

I doubted she'd put up a fight, not in her current emotional state, but that would still erode the trust Bishop and Cyrus had built with her during our journey to the death god's temple. She'd be afraid again and I couldn't stand to see her afraid.

I'll get her myself, I added before Finn could ask any questions. I didn't want to have to explain why I cared about Audrey. Sure, we'd traveled north together, but everyone knew I didn't like people and wouldn't express even a casual interest in a woman.

The terror racing through our mating bond surged, stealing my breath, and I ran as fast as I could, narrowly avoiding running into people and carts.

It didn't matter that I was making a spectacle of myself, that these pack members were seeing me for the first time in years. I had to get to her.

I barreled around a corner and climbed half a dozen stairs to the northern terrace, following the pull on my soul.

The reek of alcohol, rotting food, and piss was strong, and the street was lined with refuse. The two inns, three bars, and one brothel that took up this block still hadn't kept their part of Stonehaven clear. It was an ongoing cycle where Cyrus fined the owners, they did their part for a month and then slacked off again.

If any of them had been shifters, he could have compelled them, but the inns and bars were owned by humans and the brothel by a Dedearc — a being supposedly originating from the mythical dragons and demons — and our alpha power didn't work on them.

The pull jerked me toward a narrow alley between the last bar on the row and a blocky two-story building with a clothier on the first floor.

There. Audrey was there.

I raced to the alley's mouth afraid of what I'd find—

Fuck! It was worse than I could have imagined.

She stood at the back of the alley beside a dented garbage bin, screaming and sobbing, and swinging a broken bottle as if she were being attacked.

Blood poured from her body and pooled beneath her feet. Her left arm had been cut so many times it was impossible to tell if her injuries were a few deep cuts or dozens of shallow ones. More cuts sliced through her dress over her left breast and across her right thigh as well as a few shallow ones close to the artery in her neck that turned my panic into frozen horror.

"Get out," she cried, tears leaking from her closed eyes as I raced to get to her. "Get out, get out, get out."

With a scream, she slashed the broken bottle across her already bloody left forearm then jerked as if she'd been struck and sucked in a sharp breath. Her eyelids fluttered open, her expression dazed, then her gaze slowly dragged down her body to the bottle, her ruined dress, and the too-large pool of blood around her feet.

"Sterling," she gasped, saying the name of one of the monsters from her old pack who'd tried to kill her.

Horror flooded our bond then her eyes rolled back.

"No!" I leaped toward her, shifting into my human form, and caught her before she crumpled to the ground.

There was so much blood. Too much blood. I could feel her life draining out of her as I clutched her to my chest.

My mate was dying. I didn't know what had happened, but I'd failed her.

I'd. Failed. Her.

BISHOP

A HEART-STOPPING MIX OF RAGE AND PANIC SHOT THROUGH my bond with Knox, making my knees buckle. With a growl, I slammed my shoulder against the alley wall and managed to stay upright while only staggering up the remaining uneven steps to reach the top of the northern terrace then kept running.

Knox had said Audrey was in trouble, his worry so strong he'd let his full power slip — or maybe even released it on purpose — something he never did. Eloise and Kira, our cook and her assistant, had dropped to their knees from the force of his power, and I had a feeling so had everyone in a two-hundred-foot radius from Knox since Cyrus had then been inundated with telepathic questions about what was going on.

Another full blast hit me, compelling me to hurry and help, and Knox screamed in my head.

"Oh, Sisters," Nova gasped. "Was that—?"

"Knox?" I said. "Yeah."

"Finn says he sees them. Northgate Road. Nova," Cyrus barked with a leak of power. "You need to shift and meet them at the closest med pack."

"Corner of Northgate and Menders," Nova said as she shifted into her small, white and reddish-brown wolf, not even pausing to take off her dress. Then she raced out of the alley and onto a narrow, unnamed street heading toward Northgate.

I shifted as well and ran after her. While we'd traveled to the death god's temple, the betas had set up medical packs in secure locations all over town — the majority on the perimeter — and started voluntary first aid classes for anyone who wanted to know how to use what was in the packs. We'd lost too many people in the grimalkin attack and Nova had sworn it wouldn't happen again.

I could only pray that Finn had been in one of the first few classes, or that there was someone else nearby who could help since Knox didn't know a whole lot of first aid and, from the panic racing through our bond, was barely holding it together.

What the hell had happened? And why the hell had Audrey been roaming Stonehaven alone?

For the most part, the town was safe, but she was a very weak, very pretty female and even in the nicest parts of town she could have drawn males too eager for her attention and unwilling to listen to her soft, shy requests to be left alone. That she'd ended up on the north side of Stonehaven, the shadiest part of town with the foreigners not beholden to an alpha, had me even more worried.

Knox, I called out, praying I was close enough to reach him.

She's dying, he screamed back. *She— Bishop, I can't— It's just like when we found her in the river.*

Someone attacked her? My wolf rose to the surface and seized control. We'd kill whoever had hurt her, tear him to pieces and bathe in their blood.

I don't know. There wasn't anyone around. She wasn't even awake when she hurt herself.

She hurt herself? How—?

I. Don't. Know! he roared, his desperation and panic crashing through me, propelling me faster.

With my longer legs, I passed Nova even though I had no idea which building had the Northgate Menders med pack.

But it didn't matter. Knox's fear was a physical, impossible pull on our bond, drawing me to him — something that had never happened before. I wasn't even sure how it was possible, because there wasn't a bond strong enough to tell someone where the other was.

I sped out of another narrow no-name street and climbed the shallow steps onto Menders, a wider street that joined the northern terrace with the rest of the town. I passed a group of people frozen from the power pouring off Knox, caught in the opposing compulsions to help and to get away. Beyond them, I could see Knox at the next intersection. Menders and Northgate.

He knelt on the ground, clutching a limp Audrey to his chest while Finn knelt beside him, pulling stuff out of a bright yellow duffle bag. Blood darkened the ground around them in a too-large pool and there were already two elixir ampules lying discarded on the ground.

I slid to a stop beside them and shifted into my human form, taking a handful of gauze from Finn and clamping it down on Audrey's mutilated left forearm.

A second later, Nova appeared and nudged me to the side so she could get at Audrey.

"Save her," Knox growled, clutching Audrey tighter.

"I will," she said, meeting Knox's dark gaze, her expression tight with worry and determination. "I promise. But you have to put her down."

Knox trembled and the muscles in his arms flexed. Power rolled off him, commanding me to save her, now now now, and the panic in our bond stole my breath.

"I can't," he gasped. "I can't. Nova, please."

"I've already given her the pack's two elixirs," Finn said.

"Who did this?" Cyrus demanded, his own power vibrating at the edge of my senses, his control on the verge of slipping.

He was going to kill whoever had hurt her. It was clear in his eyes. But there was also something deeper, darker in his gaze. I couldn't recognize the emotion, but it made my already churning insides cold with dread.

Nova peeled back the gauze, revealing the mess of Audrey's arm then slapped the gauze back down and moved to the gauze Finn held over her chest and thigh.

"I don't know," Knox replied, his attention locked on Audrey's pale face, his body trembling. "I saw her cut herself. She was standing and crying and cutting herself with a broken bottle."

All the color drained from Cyrus's face and he jerked a step closer.

Knox tensed. "Too close," he growled, his voice low, his breathing suddenly sharp and ragged, the surge of fear that marked a panic attack bursting through our bond. "You're too close. All of you are too close!"

Cyrus heaved himself back, and Finn and I inched as far away as we could while still holding the gauze in place. No one wanted to risk Knox's wolf losing it, and while Finn didn't know we'd just barely saved him from going feral a few hours ago, he sure as hell remembered how vicious Knox had been the last time.

Knox sucked in a sharp breath then another and squeezed his eyes tight. I could feel him struggling to not let his fear overwhelm him. Even his wolf was helping, fighting against the most primal part of its nature to stay in control because that was the only way to help Audrey.

"I think she was asleep," Knox forced out. "She looked so surprised."

"I need to stitch most of this," Nova said as she taped the gauze around Audrey's forearm then ripped the front of Audrey's dress so she could tape gauze there as well. "But I want to do a thorough cleaning first. The elixirs will help, but I'd rather she wasn't also fighting an infection on top of trying to heal this degree of damage."

Another burst of panic swept through our bond and Knox's grip on Audrey tightened.

"I need to be with her," he said.

Finn's eyebrows shot up at that announcement but he thankfully didn't say anything. As it was, people were going to be talking. Knox had frozen every shifter in the immediate area, locking them in his fear to avoid crowds and his desperation to save his mate.

Before the day was done, everyone was going to know that Knox and Audrey were mate bonded. There was no other logical explanation for his reaction. And everyone was going to be wondering how and why it had happened. The wolf that didn't need or want anyone now had a mate. One who couldn't even shift and live the same lifestyle as him.

"We'll set up something outside her suite," Cyrus assured him. "Finn. Run ahead until you're close enough. Tell Whil to meet us in the gold suite and get Zavier to set up a mattress on the patio. Last time I saw him, he was with Lucius in the library."

"Yes, alpha," he said, thankfully without asking the questions that I could see in his confused expression. He yanked off his shirt, dropped his pants, and raced away, shifting mid-step.

"You think there's more going on?" I asked Cyrus, as he gathered up Finn's clothes and shoved the gauze, tape, and empty ampules back in the med pack. There wasn't any other reason for him to summon Whil.

"She didn't sleepwalk the entire time we were traveling. I don't know why she'd start now," he replied, leading us back toward the Residence. "She was caught up in a spell that ripped a hole between her realm and ours, and her heat was a lot stronger than it should have been for someone so weak."

Nova shot him a dark look. "And trauma can do strange things to a person. She's in a mate bond she didn't expect, just survived a dangerous and exhausting journey, and doesn't yet know her place in this pack. Anything could have been the last straw for her. Any *sharp words* could have pushed her subconscious over the edge."

Cyrus stiffened at that. Something had happened, and if I knew Cyrus, she'd done something to make him panic — like she'd done for most of our journey — and with the stress of Knox going feral, he'd lost it.

Sudden fury blazed through my bond with Knox.

"You did this?" he demanded, his eyes dark and his canines extended as his wolf took over. "You made our mate hurt herself?"

A crack of his power made me and Nova stumble while Audrey whimpered and the rage in the bond jerked back to fear.

"We'll find out what happened and we'll deal with it," Cyrus said.

We ran through the Residence's main gate and skirted around the castle, not bothering to navigate the maze of hallways to get to Audrey's suite. Zavier and Lucius had already set up a mattress with pillows and blankets on the small, semi-private patio that was sheltered by some tall shrubs and planter boxes. Beside it, was a white sheet and a low table with the medical supplies Nova needed to clean Audrey's wounds, stitch them up, and rebind them.

Knox sat on the white sheet, laying Audrey so her head was cradled in his lap. It still wasn't the space Nova needed to work, but it was better than clutching Audrey to his chest, and Nova didn't comment on the position.

Nova had cornered me when I'd first gotten back to Stonehaven and demanded to know what had happened between Audrey and Knox, and I'd told her they'd been forced to seal the bond.

I could only assume since Deacon had known about the mate bond and that we'd been traveling to the death god's temple to break it, that he'd told Nova, since the only other person who'd known about it when we'd left town, was Whil, and she'd sworn to keep it a secret.

Of course, now it didn't matter. Everyone knew and everyone was going to be talking about it.

Nova got to work cutting Audrey out of her dress and cleaning the gashes on her left breast, right over her heart.

What had she been trying to do? Cut her heart out? Cut out her bond with Knox?

She'd been so strong for the journey to the death

god's temple and I'd thought, even though she'd been shaken by the heat fever, that she was all right. She'd been upset and shyer than she'd been when we'd first met, but I hadn't thought she was suicidal, not even on an unconscious level.

Maybe Cyrus was right. Maybe, somehow, she'd been influenced by magic.

Whil and Finn hurried around the shrubs, and Knox tensed at the additional people before Finn, Lucius, Cyrus, and I stepped back.

"What happened?" Whil asked, her bright green gaze sweeping over Audrey and taking in the blood and gauze and her still too-thin frame.

It broke my heart to see her so fragile because I knew she wasn't fragile. Someone had just convinced her she was. And while I didn't know the extent of what she suffered in her previous pack, I knew enough to know she wouldn't have survived if she'd truly been fragile. She also wouldn't have survived the attack that had brought her to us, the journey to the death god's temple, or a heat fever.

"We're not sure," Cyrus replied, making Knox growl, the sound low and threatening. The muscles in Cyrus's jaw flexed and his spine straightened just a little bit more, revealing his discomfort. "We need you to check her for magical influence."

"I didn't notice anything when I checked her when she first arrived," Whil said as she sat on Audrey's other side and placed a hand on her forehead. "Oh, Sisters!"

Cyrus flinched as if he wanted to get closer then remembered that we needed to give Knox space. "What?"

"She's tethered to someone," Whil replied.

"Who?" I asked.

"I don't know. They're far away. I swear the tether wasn't there a month ago." Whil closed her eyes to concentrate and her magic brightened enough for me to see the golden glow around her hand even in the bright sunlight.

"It's that asshole," Knox said. "The one that tried to kill her. It has to be."

"And he could have made her hurt herself with this connection?" Cyrus asked.

The glow flared, washing out Audrey's already pale face and Whil frowned. "It could make her do lots of things," she replied. "But she'd have to be vulnerable to start with. This isn't strong enough to possess her. She'd have to already have emotions toward whatever they wanted her to do and then they could amplify it out of proportion."

Which meant Audrey might not have been stressed and depressed enough to hurt herself, but the seed had been there.

Cyrus hissed a curse and ran his hand over his face, his "alpha-in-control" mask sliding over his expression. Her being connected to someone had more repercussions than just her hurting herself.

What if she got mad at one of us? Could whoever it was influence her into hurting someone else? Maybe even kill them? Now it was a matter of protecting not just Audrey but the whole pack.

"Can you cut the tether?" Cyrus asked, his voice gruff.

"I—" Whil's expression tightened and her body tensed.

The glow from her magic surrounded Audrey's head, making it difficult to make out her features, and a second later, Audrey cried out and started writhing.

"Whil!" Knox snapped, holding Audrey's head and keeping it in his lap, as Nova threw herself over Audrey's body to keep her still, and I grabbed Audrey's legs.

"Just— I—" Tears rolled down Whil's cheeks, her body clenched with effort, and the light started to stutter, sharp, piercing strobes that sliced into my brain.

Please let her cut it. Please let Audrey be free. I could protect her from a lot of things and I wanted to with all my heart, but I couldn't protect her from someone in her head. Even if we were mate bonded, I wouldn't be able to do that.

"I can't," Whil gasped as she threw herself back, leaning against the side of the mattress gasping for air as Audrey went limp again. "I've blocked it, so whoever it is can't influence her again, for now, but I can't sever it. I'm not strong enough."

Cyrus gave a tight nod and Knox's emotions soured inside me.

Yeah, I didn't like the "for now," either.

"I'll need to check the block regularly to keep it intact," Whil said.

"For how long?" Knox asked.

Her expression turned grim. "Indefinitely."

Which meant that monster was going to be haunting Audrey for the rest of her life.

AUDREY

I WOKE GROGGY AND SORE AND STRANGELY AT PEACE. Warmth radiated around my heart and every breath was filled with the comforting scent of wood smoke.

For some reason, I was outside on a soft mattress bundled in blankets that smelled smoky like Knox, but I couldn't figure out why. In front of me, I could see French doors that looked a lot like the doors in my suite, but it was too dark — the sky barely lightening with dawn — for me to tell if I was actually on the patio outside my suite or not.

Behind me, something big and heavy and warm pressed against my back, like how Bishop used to curl around me when we cuddled around the campfire, but there weren't any arms around me so it couldn't have been a person, and I was too woozy to bother moving to see what it actually was. I just wanted to lie there, wrapped in the warmth, feeling safe.

But the memories flooded in.

The fear and rage of Knox's emotions through our mate bond as his wolf tried to consume the human half of his soul. The terror when I'd fallen into the arena and he'd charged at me, and my relief when his wolf finally released him. Then Cyrus had yelled at me, shown who he really was, and proven I wasn't safe in Stonehaven. I wasn't safe anywhere.

Except was that really true?

Cyrus had been gruff and looked down on me for not being able to do much of anything, but he'd never been cruel. Even when he'd been yelling at me, I'd seen the worry in his eyes... I just hadn't realized I'd seen it at the time.

I'd been so focused on the similarities between him and Merrick when Merrick had first taken me in, and I'd been scared that my nightmares had been right, that the guys were using me, that I should be ashamed for how I'd behaved during my heat. That I was worthless and trapped.

My throat tightened, the fear and shame swelling and threatening to strangle me.

I thought I was stronger than that, that I could wait and plan and stay unnoticed. I thought things had finally changed.

No. They *had* changed.

Without the pressure of Knox's emotions and being exhausted from traveling for close to a month, the bleakness that had overwhelmed me when Cyrus had yelled at me was gone. How could I have thought Bishop was using me?

Because I'd trusted the false mating call and believed Royce would love me. I couldn't trust my own judgment. I was too easily tricked and manipulated.

No.

I squeezed my eyes shut and sucked in more deep breaths of Knox's comforting scent.

I'd been manipulated because of magic. No one would have suspected Royce and Sterling would have hired a witch to fake a mating call. No one would have suspected anyone of doing that.

I could trust Bishop, and even though Knox had really hurt me when he rejected me, the bond was sealed. I could trust him. Even if we weren't in love now, we would be... eventually. The bond would see to that. It didn't matter if I feared that he couldn't possibly love me. That fear was wrong. He'd said he'd try with us and I believed him... or did I just want to believe him?

Gah! This was so frustrating.

I. Could. Trust. Them.

Neither Bishop nor Knox were psychopaths. Cyrus wasn't one, either. Everything Cyrus did was to protect his pack. Knox had already hurt him, Deacon, and Bishop and was on the verge of completely losing his humanity. Even *I'd* feared that he was going to hurt me when I'd fallen into the arena.

Except even if Cyrus had been rightly afraid for me,

that didn't negate what he'd said afterward. People said what lay deep in their hearts when they finally snapped, and Cyrus had looked like he'd completely snapped. He'd meant it when he told me I couldn't just do what I wanted, that I needed to remember my place.

He might not be cruel like Merrick, but he was still an alpha, and somewhere during our trip north I'd forgotten that, forgotten how I was supposed to behave. Even if he and his brothers hadn't cared while we'd been alone, we were back in the pack and I was the newest weakest member. My place was to be seen, not heard, and obey commands from my superiors — which included everyone in the pack.

I couldn't let my guard down around anyone until they'd proven without a doubt that I could trust them and that I was safe with them. Which meant for the time being, I could only relax around Knox and Bishop.

The realization about my safety, or lack thereof, made my thoughts jump back to Sterling and how he'd tortured me for half of my life. Even in my nightmares, I hadn't been able to escape him.

Was he always going to be stuck in my mind?

I hadn't dreamed of him when I'd first arrived in this realm. Instead, I'd had intense sexual dreams of Knox. But after the spell to break our bond had failed, my dreams of Knox had turned into nightmares of Sterling.

My thoughts stuttered. His words at the end of my latest nightmare, just before I woken and realized I'd cut myself over and over again with a broken bottle, shuddered through me.

The sacrifice is now complete.

That was what he'd wanted all along. My only use for him as a member of his pack and as a person was to feed a monster and make him more powerful.

Except I wasn't dead.

Had I somehow screwed up his plans by surviving that horrible night when I'd escaped into this realm?

I'd thought when I'd confronted him at the rip and his skin had turned red and ghostly ram's horns had appeared at his temples just like the monster that had tried to eat me, that he'd gotten the power he'd wanted. But maybe I was wrong.

The monster had eaten Merrick, but he hadn't been the one whose incomplete mating bond had been used to power the spell.

That thought made my lips twitch with a vicious smile. Weak little me might have fucked up Sterling's plans.

But my smile quickly slipped away with a new horrible realization.

If my nightmares were more than nightmares — and a big part of me felt that they were — then Sterling wasn't done with me.

I'd thought I was safe from him in this realm, that the rip was gone or too small for him to get to me, but what if I was wrong?

I might have been in a different realm when he'd used

his alpha power through the rip to control me, but my dreams were different from standing within sight of him. I hadn't even been close to the rip. It was over a day away in Anakar.

Except he'd been able to control Tzanagoth's spirits, creating those flying snake things to attack us. He had powers he'd never had before and there was no telling what else he could do. He could have used them to make me dream and think those horrible things in an attempt to kill myself and finish his ritual.

The heavy pillow behind me huffed and hot breath washed over the back of my neck.

Oh, shit. Not a pillow. I'm in bed with someone.

The panic of being in bed with a stranger squeezed my chest, and I lurched onto my back to stare into the dark brown, green-flecked eyes of an enormous black wolf.

Knox.

He nuzzled my throat, his wet nose cold against my skin and my sudden panic vanished, leaving me achy and exhausted from my ordeal. With a whimper, I rolled closer and dug my fingers into his soft fur.

I still wanted to be mad at him for hurting me when he rejected our bond, and I was determined to keep my word and make him beg for my forgiveness, but I also needed to be comforted by my mate. I was scared that Sterling could still get to me, and with Knox — just like with Bishop — my soul felt steadier, stronger.

With him, as conflicted as I was, I felt safe.

But was I? If Sterling was in my head making me dream things— hell, making me *think* things, I wasn't safe anywhere.

It wasn't you, he said, his mental voice gruff. But it wasn't gruff with anger. It was gruff with worry. And the second I realized that, I could feel his concern seeping through the bond.

"It was Sterling," I told him.

Yes. He sighed, his relief breezing through me that I realized the truth and wasn't still trying to kill myself. *He was influencing you through a magical connection.* Then he drew back to look me in the eyes. *May I hold you?*

Ahhh...?

"You're my mate. Aaaand we're already lying in a bed together." Except he wasn't in his human form which put a certain amount of distance between us.

You needed me to help you heal, he said, as if that explained why we were in a bed, outside... which it sort of did. At least the "in bed together" part. Just not the "outside" part.

But I— His gaze shifted to the edge of the hedges, but I couldn't tell if it was because he'd heard something or couldn't maintain eye contact. *I didn't know if you'd want me to hold you.*

I do, I said, my voice not nearly as strong as I wanted it to be. I needed him and I wasn't going to think too hard about it. "I'm still upset at you, but I—" Now it was my turn to look away. "Sterling is in my head. I'm afraid I'm never going to be free of him."

Knox shifted into his human form, revealing his lean-muscled, sculpted body before sliding under the blankets with me and pulling me to his chest.

"Whil couldn't break the connection, but she did block it."

"So I'm safe?" I asked, shivering at the feel of his body pressed against mine.

"Yes," he replied, but I could feel his hesitation through our mating bond.

"It's not just yes, is it?"

He frowned. "So you can feel my emotions, too. It's not just me?" he asked instead.

"It's not just you and don't change the subject." I didn't want to make demands of an alpha. I couldn't force him to tell me anything even if I was his mate, but I needed to know what he wasn't telling me. "I need to know."

"Whil will need to regularly reinforce the block," he said.

"How regularly?" And for how long?

Except I had a feeling I already knew. It was going to be for however long Sterling or I lived.

"She doesn't know. But it's not a mating or soul bond in any way. There will be ways to break it," he replied, tightening his grip around me.

"Swell." I felt like I was back where I started a month ago, with a connection I needed to break and no easy way to do it... because if there was an easy way, Whil would have done it already.

"I promise," Knox said, his grip around me tightening as if he could keep me safe from my own head by just holding me tighter. "You'll be free of him even if I have to find a way to your realm and kill him."

A surge of violent determination swept through the bond. Yeah, a part of me wanted to go back to watch that, but according to everything Whil and Bishop had told me, returning to my realm was impossible.

"Whil is confident you can have a normal life," Knox insisted. "Do what you want... with who you want."

A shiver of desire swept down my spine and Knox groaned, reminding me that we could feel each other's emotions.

"I'm sorry," I murmured, embarrassment heating my cheeks.

"You don't apologize," he growled. "*I* apologize."

He brushed his lips against my jaw, the tenderness of his touch surprising and feeding the warmth of our shifter connection around my heart. With the exception of when we were huddling together for warmth after he'd rescued me from the flash flood, all my interactions with Knox — at least all that I could remember — were brusque, distant, or angry.

Nothing between us had been tender like it was between me and Bishop. Even the Knox in my dreams had been wild and ferocious. And while Bishop and Knox were identical twins with only a few subtle differences to tell them apart, I knew in my soul Knox was the one kissing me, not Bishop.

Except now that I focused on his kiss, it felt less tender and compassionate and more careful, as if he were afraid of hurting me... or me rejecting him.

AUDREY

"Knox—" I began, but I didn't know what to say. My soul yearned to reassure him, remind him that we were mates and that I'd never reject him. But my brain was still angry at him for doing exactly that to me.

"You almost died," he said, his lips brushing across my jaw to find my mouth. "I wasn't there to protect you and you almost—" He growled, the sound a low rumble in his chest. "Never again. I'll figure it out. Somehow. You're mine and I protect what's mine."

Ah. So he wasn't being tender because he was afraid of me rejecting him. He was afraid because I was so weak.

I wanted to yell at him that I wasn't weak, but Sterling had once again proven that I was. Even my mind was weak, easily manipulated.

God, I was so sick and tired of the same thoughts running through my head over and over again. I didn't want to be weak. I might not have any power and might not be able to shift, but I could be strong. Humans were strong, or at least stronger than me. They didn't have any magic and weren't simpering doormats. Some of them knew how to stand up for themselves and I wanted to be like that. I yearned for that.

Except every time I tried something, I was slapped back down and reminded of my place. And I couldn't afford to forget that, not now when I couldn't escape this pack.

Knox deepened our kiss, his desire and determination seeping through our mate bond, and he skimmed his hand down my throat, under my blanket, and along the top of my right breast, so close to my nipple and yet oh so far away.

A shiver of need pebbled the tiny bud, making him smile into our kiss, and I felt his pleasure at my pleasure swell between us. It was a complete circuit, both of us feeding off each other, our need building with each stroke of his tongue against mine and each brush of his fingers over my aching flesh.

Except I wanted to be strong about something. Anything. And giving in to Knox the second an intimate moment present itself wasn't standing up for myself.

I'd told him I was going to make him beg. If I gave in now, he'd know he could always get what he wanted with a kiss and a gentle touch.

"Knox," I gasped, pushing his mouth away from mine. "I'm not giving you sex."

He stared at me, his gaze capturing mine, concern

sliding through the desire coming from him along with a hint of surprise as if he didn't understand why I'd pushed him away.

"I'm still mad at you for hurting me."

"You should be." He frowned and for a second it felt like he was reaching through our bond and sifting through all my emotions. "But you're not. You're determined."

He rose onto one elbow to better stare into my eyes and his hand on my breast shifted, the edge of his fingers brushing my nipple and sliding soft heat to my core.

"And you want me to keep touching you," he said slowly as if he couldn't understand my emotions.

"I told you'd I'd resist you. That—"

"That you'd make me beg," he said, cutting me off. "Even if it goes against what you want?"

"Not having sex won't hurt me," I huffed, even though a part of me was starting to ache for him, for the glorious sensations that made all the other complicated, painful emotions, go away. "You thinking you can always get what you want does hurt me. I've already lived that life, trapped with alphas that didn't care what I wanted. I won't go back to that." I swallowed at the lump in my throat. "I can't." Not with my mate.

My voice broke on the last word and Knox pulled me into his arms, hugging me to his chest, his tenderness surprising me... but then he'd held me after I'd almost drowned as well, giving me strength through our shifter connection and our mating bond.

"You won't go back to that. I promise. I didn't mean to hurt you," he said, his voice gruff, his desire softening and turning into something heartbreakingly sad. "I'm broken. I didn't want you stuck with me."

"I know you were trying to protect me." But I'd only realized that truth when I'd begged his wolf to let the human half of his soul go and figured out that he'd gone so far as to collar his wolf to keep us apart. It would have been so much easier, and hurt a lot less, if he'd just come out and told me. So much heartache could have been avoided.

"There's a reason we're outside on a mattress and not in the big bed in your suite. And it's not because it's a nice night," he said, his voice soft. "You were badly hurt and you needed me to steady your soul as much as I needed you to steady mine." The muscles in his jaw flexed and a whisper of panic ghosted through our bond. "But I can only be inside for a few hours. Less if I'm stressed."

The panic grew stronger as if just thinking about it scared him.

"I can't do crowds, either," he added, his fear making my breath pick up and my stomach churn. "I don't really like most people, with or without a crowd. I can't be a good mate. I can't give you a mating ceremony or spend the night with you. I can't hang out with your friends or go to events with you. That's no way to live."

I wasn't sure what to say to that. I'd thought he didn't want me because I was weak and couldn't shift, or because he was in love with someone else or afraid of commitment.

Hell, he *was* afraid of commitment, just not the way I expected.

He didn't want to commit because he thought he couldn't. And from the fear bleeding through our bond it wasn't a matter of him not wanting to do those things. He actually *couldn't*.

If we were back in my realm, he'd have access to therapists and psychiatrists — if he could be convinced to see them — and medication. In this realm, his only option for dealing with his phobia was avoidance.

I'd be a horrible person, let alone a terrible mate, if I demanded him to change. I was afraid I couldn't change from being a weakling, no matter how much I wanted to. I couldn't expect him to change, either.

This was the reality of our relationship and we were just going to have to figure it out since breaking up wasn't an option.

"It's okay," I said. "I don't need those things."

He huffed. "I know you do. I can feel it in our bond. I felt your hurt when I said we couldn't have a mating ceremony."

I wanted to deny those words, but I couldn't, and with him being able to feel my emotions, there was no point in putting up a false front.

A mating ceremony was a proclamation to the pack that we were mated. It told everyone that he wanted me and even though he was trying to protect me from unwanted questions by not having the ceremony — if he could even stand being in that type of gathering with the least amount of people possible — it still hurt. It felt like he was rejecting me all over again even though I knew he wasn't.

"It hurts because it reminds me of your rejection." My throat tightened to the point of burning, and I slid my gaze to the two moons, still visible in the lightening sky. The one moon looked like the regular moon in the mortal realm, while the other was smaller and pink, a constant reminder of everything that had happened to me and that I wasn't home and never would be.

"It's a hurt that's going to stick around," I told him truthfully even though I was afraid of his reaction. "There's a lot mixed up with it, like how sometimes I'm still that little girl who thinks no one wants her."

Knox's grip tightened and he pressed his lips against the top of my head, breathing in my scent.

"I thought it was the right thing to do." He released a shuddering breath that washed warm over my forehead and cheeks. "And I was scared. You weren't anything I planned for and it happened so fast and I can't even come close to the mate you deserve. You should have bonded with Bishop."

"But I didn't."

"You didn't," he murmured. "I'm sorry I hurt you and I swear I'll try."

His emotions churned, his fear growing stronger, but

mixed in with the fear was determination and worry and a hint of surprise.

"I don't deserve you," he said, "and I don't expect you to be anyone other than who you are." The fear in his emotions churned stronger. "But you need to talk to me. I don't want to find you like that—" The muscles in his jaw flexed and more worry slid through the bond. "I don't want to find you like that again."

"It works both ways," I told him, making him frown. "The talking part. You need to talk to me, too."

KNOX

I drew in another deep breath of Audrey's scent and held her close. I couldn't get enough of her, of the warmth around my heart from our bond and our deep shifter connection, or the feel of her tiny, fragile body protected against mine. I also couldn't get enough of her good feelings, her hope and determination and desire.

Our stronger-than-normal mating bond was an incredible blessing... but also a curse.

It went both ways and neither of us could hide from the other — since I'd already tried blocking it, like I could block my twin bond with Bishop, and failed.

For good or bad, we'd always know what the other was feeling.

The thought that I'd never be alone even in my own head worried me. I liked being alone and needed quiet even from my own thoughts. But I also liked this direct connection to Audrey's emotions. I'd never have to guess if I made her happy and I'd know right away when I screwed up.

Given how I had trouble reading subtle emotional clues, along with how Audrey was sometimes afraid to speak her mind, our bond was the only way to know when she was truly happy and content.

And speaking of happy...

I wanted to go back to the warmth of her desire. She was worried again and sad, and while Whil had said she'd blocked that asshole's influence, I didn't want a repeat of yesterday morning. The best way to prevent it was to strengthen her positive emotions so she couldn't spiral into depression and be coerced into anything again.

I slid my hand back under the blankets to her right breast — since her left was covered with gauze — and traced my fingers over her flesh, circling closer and closer to her nipple. She'd liked that before and I was rewarded with her growing desire radiating soft and warm through our bond.

"Knox, please," she said, frustration edging her voice and seeping into her emotions.

"I'm not asking for sex." Even though my wolf and my cock thought that was a great idea. "I'm *giving* you sex."

"Giving me sex, gives you sex."

"Not if you're the only one having orgasms."

She huffed and the frustration flickering through her desire bled away. She ached for me as much as I ached for her and only part of that was due to the mating bond's influence. Or at least, it was in her case.

In my case, the bond had almost nothing to do with it. She was everything my wolf desired despite his desires being contradictory. She was strong, even though it was a quiet, persistent strength that she and others didn't recognize, *and* she needed me to protect her.

The urge to wrap her in my arms and never let her go surged and she responded with a flutter of comfort, knowing, even if it was on a subconscious level, that she was safe with me. And now that I'd gotten my head out of my ass, she always would be.

She turned her head to look me in the eyes, our emotions feeding off each other, my satisfaction growing at her comfort and my desire surging with hers.

But there was still uncertainty in her eyes. It was so soft, I wouldn't have felt it in our bond if I hadn't seen it in her stunning golden-brown orbs, and all I wanted was to make it go away, to reassure her completely.

You know what we need to do, my wolf said, his need to mate with her, to feel her coming around our cock, rising to the surface.

We could probably tease her into giving us sex, but she'd said no and I intended to honor that. I needed to rise her up and give her confidence to stand against the assholes she'd inevitably come across, just like she had when she'd yelled at me on our way back to Stonehaven. Going against her wishes wouldn't accomplish that.

Then make her scream our name.

My hand dipped lower, jumping straight to her mound, and I directed it to her thigh before my wolf could plunge our fingers inside her.

Slowly. We need to go slowly, I insisted, even as her desire spiked.

She'd been unconscious for almost a whole day, and while the elixirs would have mostly healed her injuries by now, she wasn't a hundred percent. That, and as much as my hard-as-hell cock hurt, I wanted to prove myself to her and worship her.

At least let us taste her, my wolf whined, thankfully not pushing me because he, too, knew Audrey needed to be loved, not fucked.

A taste was a great idea. Her scent was soft and sweet, her arousal would be the same. I just had to remember to take it slow, prove to her that I wanted to spend my time on her and that she was worth it... something I'd never done, and never felt, for a woman before.

My fingers inched higher up her thigh, dipping from the top of her leg to the inside, and I pressed my palm against her flesh to stop myself.

Slowly, I reminded my wolf as I tenderly brushed my lips along her jaw.

She turned into the kiss, her lips seeking mine, the uncertainty still a barely-there whisper in her emotions.

I feared no matter what I did, it would always be there, an ugly insidious seed her previous alpha had planted in her soul when she was a child.

Then our lips connected and she released a soft sigh,

her desire strengthening, making my soul sing. I'd done that. I'd made her forget her worries even if it was only for a second, and I was determined to make her feel and forget so much more.

With a control I hadn't thought possible given the wildness of my wolf, I kissed her softly, reverently with gentle sips that, much to my surprise, built up a heated need within her.

Moaning, she leaned into me, pressing more of her body against mine, her lips growing insistent, begging me to deepen the kiss. Hints of the power locked deep within her flickered against my skin, teasing out my own power like it had in our shared dreams.

But unlike the dreams, our powers didn't fight for dominance. They swirled and danced, curling around each other, merging together then breaking apart, building building building into a heady, aching heat.

"Knox," she begged, her ache at just being kissed shocking me. I hadn't thought something so soft could be so sexual.

But then, I realized it wasn't the softness building up her need, it was the tease and our whirling emotions.

My fingers were still firmly pressed against her thigh, but if I moved an inch I'd be at the crux between her leg and mound. Less than an inch more and I could be playing with her wet heat.

My kiss had inflamed her desire for more, possibly for everything despite her earlier insistences, and my cock throbbed at the thought, precum slicking against my stomach. Except if I took advantage of her now, she'd never trust me.

I'd fucked everything up right from the start and that trust was going to be hard won. I deserved to work for it, and I would.

With a soft growl, I deepened the kiss, plunging my tongue inside her mouth and stealing her moans. Her glorious desire tingled around my heart and made my balls painfully tight, and I reveled in the sensation. I wanted her not because of the mate bond but because she was persistent and brave and kind. She'd tried to be kind to me and I'd been too blinded by my fear to accept her.

Never again. I swear by the Sisters. Never again.

I let all my desire for her pour through our mating bond, not wanting her to have any doubts about how I felt. It was just a fraction of what I needed to do to make it up to her, but it was a start and better than just talking to her.

I kissed her until she was breathless and trembling, then swept my lips down her neck to my mating mark, a shimmering white scar on her shoulder where I'd claimed her and sealed our bond.

It should have been the only scar on her body and not just because shifters healed fast enough to not scar with the exception of a mating mark, but because she shouldn't have had to suffer like she had.

I swept my tongue over the mark and was rewarded with a full body shiver than raced from her head to her toes along with a billow of heated need through our bond.

"Knox," she gasped, bucking her hips, trying to get me to move my fingers up her thigh. "You're killing me."

Her words brought a feral grin to my lips that I hid by dipping down to her breast and flicking my tongue over her nipple. I was beginning to understand why Bishop liked foreplay so much. It hadn't made sense to me or my wolf, but with a direct link to Audrey's emotions, I could feel her growing need, the achy, squirmy desire getting tighter and tighter, and knew I could make her see stars without pushing my cock into her.

And gods, I wanted her to feel so good she did see stars.

I doubled my effort on my teasing, sucking her nipple into my mouth and laving it with my tongue while inching my fingers closer and closer to her core. I concentrated on her, listening to her breath pick up then start to catch, feeling her body twitch and shiver, and feeling her need in our bond turn into an inferno before pulling away.

"Knox, please," she gasped, digging her fingers into my hair, her arms trembling. But it was like she couldn't decide if she wanted to hold me closer to her breast or push me away.

I decided for her and kissed my way down her belly, teasing my tongue into her belly button and nudging her thighs with my palms, asking for entrance.

She accepted me with a trembling sigh, her legs

falling open, and I settled between them, drawing in deep breaths of her scent. It was sweet and heady, thickened by her desire and captured under the blankets with me, and as much as I wanted to be cocooned in her scent, I wanted to see her face when she came more.

I pushed the blankets off my head and shoulders, exposing Audrey's pale flesh, tight nipple, and the patch of gauze tape to her chest covering her other one to the early morning sun, watching for signs that she was uncomfortable being exposed.

But she was too caught up in her desire. There wasn't even a flicker of unease in the bond, and her gaze, now molten gold in the light, captured mine, making my breath hitch.

Sisters, she was so beautiful. I didn't know which sleeping god or goddess I'd pleased to have such a stunning mate, but I would spend every day worshiping Audrey in thanks.

Her body trembling in anticipation, I nuzzled into the soft hair covering her mound and swept my tongue over her folds, carefully avoiding her clit. But she still jerked like she'd been zapped with lightning and the desire in our bond roared into a burning frenzy.

Her fingers dug into my scalp and my wolf flashed her a satisfied grin at the possessive move.

Mine. Mine mine mine.

And hers. Forever.

I trailed my tongue over her again and again, teasing and sucking, flicking her clit and pushing inside her. Her desire was the sweetest nectar, coating my tongue and filling my nose and her gasps and moans the sweetest music.

The whirl of her need propelled me forward. It was like a drug. If I licked here, she'd shudder and moan. If I backed off for a moment then licked again, her moan would be louder. I brought her to the edge of climax again and again, building the tension within her until she was begging for release.

"Knox, please," she moaned, her body strung tight, hanging on the precipice.

With a growl from my wolf, I pushed my tongue inside her, fucking her even higher, then sucked on her clit.

Audrey screamed and white-hot pleasure shot through the bond. Her body convulsed, her eyes squeezed tight and her mouth hung open. The pleasure filling her expression was glorious.

I came hard, shooting hot jets of cum onto the mattress, and didn't care. Audrey had seen stars. I didn't need to ask. The emotions rushing through our bond told me everything, and I'd never been so satisfied to not have gotten my cock wet in my life.

AUDREY

I woke to a gentle hand on my shoulder and Nova's soft voice calling my name.

"Hey," she said as she sat on the edge of the bed and I blinked sleepily at her. "How are you feeling?"

Amazing. Boneless. Thoroughly satisfied. I hadn't orgasmed so hard in my life.

And to know my pleasure had also brought Knox pleasure was empowering. I'd feared knowing what he felt would be distracting or worse, overwhelming by not knowing where my emotions ended and his began. But it had enhanced everything, a feedback loop that had just kept building and building with glorious pleasure.

After I'd seen stars and the universe and everything, Knox had carried me inside, saying he could handle a few hours before the walls closed in on him. He'd helped steady my boneless and still-trembling body as we cleaned up in the shower then held me until I fell asleep.

He'd warned me that he wouldn't be able to stay and he hadn't. The space behind me where he'd been was cold which meant he'd been gone for a while.

A whisper of disappointment that I was alone in bed curled within me but I shoved it down. It wasn't his fault. I'd felt his growing unease as we'd cuddled even though we hadn't been inside for very long, and I could tell he was trying to hide it from me.

That was just who he was and I had to accept that, just like he had to accept I was a shifter who couldn't shift.

Except that wasn't what Nova was asking me about. She didn't know Knox had given me an earth-shattering orgasm or that we'd cuddle in bed until I passed out. She was asking about my new scars, the ones that had been under the gauze patches that Knox had peeled away in the shower.

How *was* I feeling?

Better and yet not better.

Most of the weight and shame and grief since waking from the heat fever was gone, although not all of it. I didn't doubt that Bishop cared for me and the fear that he was using me and would throw me away when he was done was also gone.

But I was still wary of Cyrus and every other pack member... including Nova. Not because I thought Cyrus would hurt or punish me to the extent Merrick or Sterling had, but because there was still a chance he would reprimand me with more than just words next time. That, and he'd made it clear he didn't like weaknesses and I was a weakness.

It would be best if I just stayed out of sight and not remind him that I was permanently bound to his family, as well as keep a low profile from the rest of the pack, let them know I knew my place at least until I'd proven that I wasn't worthless. Hopefully, everyone would just leave me alone.

On the other hand, I was ashamed and embarrassed that Sterling had manipulated me again. How long had he been whispering poison into my soul? And how long until Whil's magical block broke and he was influencing me again?

Except the only thing I could do about it was to pay attention to when my thoughts turned dark and ask Whil to remake the block.

I sighed. Always being on guard and hiding from everyone was no way to live, but, at the moment, it was the only way I had.

"I'm okay," I told her hesitantly, deciding okay was the safest, least complicated response I could give her.

She raised an eyebrow at that.

Guess "not complicated" wasn't a satisfactory response.

But what else could I say? Nova had been kind to me, but she'd grown up and was close friends with Bishop, Knox, and Cyrus. I needed to be careful what I said to her. At least until I was certain I could trust her.

"I ah... I spent a month walking and the spell failed,

and I ah... have a mate who's..." How did I politely sum up Knox yet still sound truthful? I couldn't lie to her. She knew better than me that Knox had issues.

"Complicated?" Nova supplied as she motioned for me to sit up. "You have a complicated mate."

"Sure. Let's go with complicated." And hot and moody and fierce and good with his mouth and difficult. "I have a mate bond neither of us wanted and I'm... ah... not sure how I can be useful to the pack."

I sat up, holding the sheet to my breasts to keep myself covered even though I knew she wanted to look at my injuries. Thankfully she didn't comment on the fact that I hadn't told her anything about my situation that she didn't already know or about my modesty. From what I'd seen of this pack, nudity wasn't something to be embarrassed about and most shifters weren't.

Only my pack, which had cursed ourselves generations ago to prevent us from shifting before after our eighteenth birthday had human-levels of modesty. And since my wolf hadn't awakened and I'd never shifted, I'd never been nude in public before.

"So, yeah," Nova replied with a wry smile. "Okay. Sounds about right." She looked at the new, pink scars on my left breast and on my left inner arm. "These have healed nicely. You should soak in the bath for a few minutes so it's easier to take the stitches out."

And then it'd be back to how it was when I'd first arrived: me needing to figure out my place in this pack and prove my worthiness. Except I needed to be careful how I went about doing it, certainly more careful with how I interacted with people than before.

Which wasn't entirely true. I was now fully mated to Knox and Bishop had promised to court me. I wasn't back to nothing.

Still, I didn't want my identity to revolve around the men in my life. I could be more than just someone's mate, no matter what Merrick or Sterling or all the others said about me.

"So, Cyrus mentioned you might be interested in joining a first aid class," Nova said as she hurried ahead of me to the bathroom and started filling the tub. "He said you knew the basics and didn't panic at the sight of blood."

I glanced around for a robe but didn't see one and didn't want to grab something from the wardrobe and change when I was only going to undress again as soon as I got to the bath.

"It wasn't anything special," I said, contemplating wrapping myself in the sheet then deciding to just suck it up.

Nova wouldn't care that I was naked *and* she was a doctor, so I clenched my jaw, trying to keep my insecurities from overwhelming me, and shuffled on still slightly weak legs to the bathtub.

"Your ability to shift eliminates the risk of infection so there isn't a lot to worry about," I said. I'd bandaged a few of Knox's deeper wounds after our first fight with a pack of jackals, but it hadn't been anything anyone else couldn't have done.

"Still, if you're interested, I have a class in a few days that's going through how and when to use everything in the emergency medical packs we've placed all over town. I wouldn't say no to anyone who wants to learn about them."

Worry darkened her expression and I could just imagine what she was thinking. Too many people had been seriously hurt and killed when that pack of grimalkins had attacked the town. She wanted anyone and everyone able to help save lives if it ever happened again.

And so did I. Maybe someone could have saved those children the grimalkin had killed. I'd managed to save four of them, and the other two had looked dead, but maybe they hadn't been. Maybe some of the pack's magical elixir would have saved them.

"Sure." I sank into the tub, letting the warm water lap up to my chin to ensure the stitches on my chest were submerged while Nova perched on the edge of the large tub and thankfully looked away to give me privacy. "I'll take the class."

I just hoped this was a hands-on class and didn't involve a textbook like the classes back home since I couldn't read their language. Which was something else I was going to have to take care of sooner rather than later.

But Bishop had said he'd help me with that so now I

just needed to remember to bring it up whenever I saw him next.

"Knox said you weren't aware that you'd hurt yourself," Nova said. "You want to tell me what happened?"

Not really. But she'd asked and not answering her could make her angry since she was my superior in the pack, something I should have been thinking about from the moment I'd first met her a month ago.

"I'm not really sure," I replied, trying to keep the hesitation from my voice.

Except that was only half the truth. After our shower, while snuggling in bed, Knox had told me that Sterling had manipulated my dreams and he'd been able to make me hurt myself because I'd already been afraid and sad and desperate. But I wasn't sure how much I wanted to confess to Nova. If she knew about my weaknesses, she could use them against me.

Except that had been true in my previous pack. It might not be true with this one.

Thinking both packs were the same was Sterling's doing. Nova had already been kind to me, and while I didn't have definitive proof I could trust her, I wanted to give her a chance.

I wanted to give everyone a chance.

Which was ridiculously naive of me, but I couldn't help myself. My old pack had decided I was useless before I'd even had a chance to prove myself. I didn't want to make the same mistake.

"I'd been having bad dreams since I woke from the

heat fever," I told her, my heart racing as I studied her profile for any hint that I'd revealed too much.

But Nova's expression didn't darken or turn pleased. It didn't even stay the same as if she were trying to keep her emotions hidden. Instead, her lips pressed tight, her brow furrowed in concern, and a hint of her power slipped her control as if she were upset, but not necessarily angry at me.

"Cyrus mentioned the only way to break your heat was for you and Knox to seal your bond. I'm sorry for that. I know neither of you wanted it."

"What else did Cyrus tell you?" Had he talked about how I didn't know my place or that I couldn't do anything?

"Only medically pertinent information," she replied. "That your heat turned into a fever and went longer than normal and way beyond what was safe. We're going to need to watch out for that in about six months when you have your next heat just in case it wasn't just the bond affecting you. He also said that you got some new scars on your shin from fighting a grimalkin and that you almost drowned. You seem to have bad luck when it comes to beasts, monsters, and fast-moving water."

That was an understatement. So far, I was 0-2 for falling in rivers and nearly drowning and 2-5 in the monster department with only two wins because I hadn't actually fought any of the jackals.

Or was I 2-7? Did psychopathic Sterling count as a

monster? I mean, I knew he was a monster, but physically he was just a shifter.

"Yeah," I agreed, dropping my gaze in case she looked at me.

"We're going to have to keep an eye on you," she added

I didn't know if she meant that in a caring way or a controlling way, and the thought sent a shiver rushing down my spine.

"Audrey," Nova said, her posture tensing as if she'd seen my shiver. "It's understandable that you've had bad dreams. You're from another realm. Things work differently here and you're alone and surrounded by strangers. I'd be shocked if you didn't have doubts or fears that haunt your dreams. It's understandable that someone magically connected to you could amplify them." She stood and grabbed a large towel from the rack near the tub, her tone softening. "No one is upset at what happened. We're just worried about you and want to keep you safe."

That was something Merrick had said when he'd first taken me in, but I didn't get the sense that Nova meant it in the same way he had. She sounded like she was genuinely concerned about me.

"So you know I'm from another realm?" I asked, hoping she wouldn't notice that I'd changed the conversation to something less personal.

She handed me the towel without looking at me.

Gratitude swelled within me that she was respecting my shyness even though she probably didn't understand it.

"Deacon got the guys to talk your first night out, and he told me when he, his hunt team, and Whil returned from Anakar," she said. "Wrap yourself in the towel and lie down on the bed so we can get those stitches out."

"Does everyone know?" I asked, obeying her instructions. Would it be good if everyone knew or would people somehow take advantage of me? It certainly would make me look like even more of a freak than I already was.

Nova grabbed her medical bag from the floor near the bedroom door and sat beside me. "Just me and Deacon and whoever else you've told."

"So only you two, Bishop, Cyrus, Knox, and Whil," I said as she pulled out her supplies then turned my left arm so it was resting comfortably on the bed and she could easily remove the stitches.

"Your hedging when I was trying to get your family history with heats makes more sense now."

"I wasn't hedging. Heats in my realm aren't like heats here." But I also hadn't told her the truth because I didn't want to become a science experiment or for her to think I was crazy and lock me up in an institution or wherever it was they locked crazy people here.

"I'd like to take some blood and monitor you," she said. "If heats don't get serious in your realm, and your first heat rose to a fever then other changes could be happening to you. It's best to try to stay on top of it."

And with one little statement, all the positive feelings I had about Nova during this conversation vanished.

"How closely do you want to monitor me?" I asked, trying to keep my fear from my voice.

"Just vitals and blood. You're not going to be an experiment," she assured me as if she knew that was one of my fears. "You have a life and a new mate who, let me tell you, is going to be a handful." She rolled her eyes at me, a lifetime of knowing Knox and his ways making her expression wry.

"He will be. But I think we'll figure it out. He's already agreed to try to make our mating work, which seems like a big deal for him."

"It's huge," she replied. "Enormous. Knox hasn't tried anything with anyone since he was a kid. For a while there, he wasn't even speaking with Cyrus and Bishop. Just basic communication with Deacon to get his solo hunting assignments."

Which didn't surprise me. Even before I'd felt the whisper of panic through our bond when Knox had mentioned he couldn't stand crowds, I knew he didn't like them. His avoiding me hadn't just been because I was an unwanted mate. It was because he didn't like social interactions with anyone.

Speaking of—

"Do you know if he's waiting outside for me?" I didn't expect him to be waiting, but if he was, I didn't want to waste his time.

"Knox had to meet with Deacon, but he told me to tell

you he'd find you after lunch," Nova said. "Don't let him take you on a long walk outside of town. You're still recovering from your injuries, your heat fever, and all that traveling. And don't let Bishop march you all around town, either. You're to stay on the Residence's grounds for the next four days, eat three meals a day plus snacks, gain some weight back, and take it easy."

She leveled a hard look at me, meeting my gaze and holding it in a show of dominance. A flicker of her power washed over me, not enough to compel me to do what she'd ordered but enough to remind me that she could.

"No leaving the Residence, eating more, and taking it easy," I repeated. "Got it."

I hadn't planned anything for the next little while. Hell, at the moment I didn't have plans for anything, not my future, or what to do about Knox and Bishop, or if I wanted to face Cyrus again or just avoid him as best I could for the rest of my life.

Staying put for the next four days was okay. Hopefully, by then I'd come up with some answers.

AUDREY

Nova finished removing the stitches from my body then waited in the living room for me to get dressed so we could go to the kitchen together and have lunch. She said it was after the usual lunchtime, but too far away from dinner to just have a snack, and given how my stomach had grumbled when she'd mentioned food, I had to agree with her.

Except now I stared at the clothes in the wardrobe, determined to ignore my reflection in the two-person, full-body mirror sitting beside it.

I had more scars and they were ragged and thick, ugly pink patches marring the flesh above my heart, my right thigh, and my left forearm. I also had new scars at the base of my neck and a few more along my ribs.

Thankfully, those ones were thin and would be less noticeable once they faded. But the other scars were always going to be obvious, just like the thick claw marks across my chest and the puncture wounds in my back and chest from the monster's claws when it had grabbed me.

Even if I could have hidden my lack of shifter power, the scars would always mark me as an anomaly. Shifters didn't scar. They healed too quickly.

Only mating bites scarred, and those were rare in my realm, and from what Bishop had told me, they were pretty rare in this realm as well.

Which meant, as much as my essence said I was a shifter to those who could sense essences, I shouldn't call myself one. I was, for all intents and purposes, a human.

Maybe if I thought of myself like that, I'd find peace. I hadn't met a lot of humans before I'd walked into Kelna, but I hadn't seemed weaker than them. In fact, if I just gained a little self-confidence, I'd probably make a decent human.

Of course, that didn't address the fact that I was still surrounded by shifters. I could be the strongest human in the realm and I'd still be weak and pathetic compared to them.

But the point was not to compare myself to them. I'd never get close and I needed to leave all the ugly things Merrick had beaten into me behind. I had a mate and another man interested in me, and I had a fresh start. People in this pack would talk and look down on me and probably hurt me just like my other pack, but I wasn't alone anymore.

I just needed to find my own path and keep out of everyone else's way.

Which was easier said than done, but true, nonetheless.

I pulled on a loose cotton shirt and pants similar to what I'd worn traveling. From what I'd seen, the outfit wasn't as common as the long, backless dresses most women wore, but I didn't want to show off more scars than necessary and I wanted to feel comfortable.

Besides, I wasn't competing with any of the women in the pack. Even if Bishop changed his mind about me — which would hurt, but wasn't something I'd fight — I still had Knox. Our relationship was still rocky, but it was permanent. The warmth radiating around my heart and the strong, sure emotions seeping through our bond reassured me.

In time, everything between us would work out. We just needed to be patient with each other.

Holding on to those feelings to keep my tentative new confidence strong, I left the bedroom.

Nova sat at the dining room table, writing in a black leather-bound notebook, but she quickly put the book and her pen into her bag and didn't keep me waiting. Beside her, the French doors were open, letting in a soft warm breeze scented with the flowers in the planter boxes and a hint of something sweet mixed with wood smoke... Knox's scent. The mattress with its rumpled blanket still sat in the middle of the small patio, and heat warmed my cheeks with the memory of what Knox and I had done last night.

"So," she said, flashing me a mischievous smile that made me smile in return despite my embarrassment. "You and Knox really are trying to make your mating work."

"We don't really have a choice," I mumbled, the heat in my face burning into my scalp and down my throat.

With her heightened senses, she could probably smell our lovemaking. There was no hiding anything from shifters.

"You don't have to have sex if you aren't sexually interested in each other... but he is handsome." She waggled her eyebrows at me, the action surprising me and making me giggle.

"He is," I replied with a sigh. "I also think once he lets his gruff standoffishness go, he'll be really sweet. I've already seen glimpses of it."

"He's just trying to protect himself," she said, leading me out of my suite and down the hall. "Also, he probably doesn't know what to do with you."

Socially, maybe. But he'd known exactly what I'd needed last night and hadn't asked for anything in return.

"He told me he's never had a relationship before."

"And very few friendships outside of his brothers. But that doesn't mean he's a bad person," Nova replied, a hint of sisterly affection seeping into her tone, reminding me that even though she wasn't technically his sister, they had grown up together and were close.

"I know. He's just shy. I can feel it." I pressed my hand over my heart. "Our bond is stronger than I expected. I can feel his emotions and he can feel mine."

"Really?" Nova's eyes widened in surprise.

A sudden flash of panic raced through me and I fought to school my expression. Had I said too much? If I'd said that to Merrick, he would have found a way to use that information against me. I didn't know how, but he would, and if Nova wasn't as trustworthy as I hoped, she could, too.

"If I hadn't thought I needed to monitor you before," she said, "I know now. Mate bonds aren't supposed to be that strong. Are they that strong in your realm?"

"No. But—" Shit. I had to tell her something. "It could be the unusual way our bond formed. And I didn't notice his emotions until we returned to Stonehaven and then on that first night Knox..." I trailed off, not sure how much more I should share. Almost going feral seemed like a really personal thing and Knox was a very private man.

"And Knox almost went feral," Nova finished for me. "A high stress situation can strengthen a bond. It's why Bishop and Knox are so deeply connected."

I waited for her to say more, but she didn't. Guess whatever happened to the twins to deepen their connection wasn't Nova's story to tell and one of them would either tell me himself or not at all. I wasn't going to push the matter. It sounded like it was serious and life-altering and I didn't want them to relive their trauma.

Sometimes it was better to just leave the past in the past.

Nova led me out of the maze of halls through the Residence's grand foyer with its sweeping staircase and massive crystal chandelier and to the kitchen. She'd mentioned that it was past lunch so it didn't surprise me that there wasn't anyone preparing food like there'd been yesterday morning.

What did surprise me were Bishop and Velora sitting at the kitchen table with open file folders, leather-bound books, and an explosion of loose papers covering the surface.

"Audrey!" Bishop exclaimed the second I stepped inside. "How are you feeling?"

He rushed around the table to reach me and cupped my cheeks with his large palms. His warm brown gaze locked with mine as if he were seeing into my soul and learning whatever was wrong with me without me telling him. Warmth and joy rushed through me — and not just because of our shifter connection.

He was genuinely pleased to see me and concerned about my well-being.

Of course, he'd always been pleased and concerned when it came to me. I didn't know how I'd doubted his intentions.

Except I did know.

I was afraid I was unlovable.

My life so far had proven I was unlovable, and to have someone like Bishop, someone beautiful and powerful,

to express interest in me went beyond my wildest
dreams.

I might not be able to trust anyone else in the pack,
especially not his oldest brother, but I could trust Bishop.

"I'm okay." I leaned into his touch and let my eyes
drift shut. Our shifter connection blended with the heat
from my mating bond, swelled around my heart, and
flooded my chest.

"She's healed, but she's still recovering," Nova said,
her tone stern. "That means no tromping around town
and wearing her out. She's to say on the Residence's
grounds for four days."

"I can carry her," Bishop shot back. "She won't have to
walk anywhere."

"It's only four days and there's plenty to do around the
Residence that doesn't risk exhausting her." A hint of
Nova's power leaked from her control, not-so-subtly
telling Bishop how serious she was about me resting.
"She can look at the gardens or meditate in the sacred
grove. Whil would probably appreciate a little company
from someone who isn't asking for something and there
are all the public rooms in the Residence that she can
explore. The library, the music room as well as the sauna
and pool on the lower level."

"We also have a gym," Bishop added.

"Which you won't use until your four days of rest are
over," Nova told me.

"I'm sure I'll need more than four days to see everything," I assured her. That and I needed to do some

serious thinking about my future. I needed to figure out how I could be useful and be worthy of being mated to one — maybe two — of the pack's alphas... I just wasn't sure how to do that because it needed to be really good to make me stand out.

"But first," Nova added. "Lunch."

She turned toward the fridge and cupboards, but Bishop cleared his throat and stopped her.

"I've already got lunch covered. I was just waiting for you to wake up," he said as he dipped close and brushed his lips across my forehead.

Nova crossed her arms and glared at him. "It better not involve taking her into town."

"It doesn't," Bishop replied, beaming at her, clearly pleased with his lunch plans. "Grab the picnic basket from the fridge, will you?"

"Bishop," Velora said, tapping her pen on the papers in front of her and shooting me an angry glare. "We need to get this done. The summer festival is only six days away."

"It's waited most of a month," he replied as Nova got a wide wooden basket with a short handle out of the fridge and he grabbed a blanket from a cupboard in the corner. "It can wait a few more hours. Deal with what we've already finished or take a break."

"The sooner we get it done, the sooner we can slow down," she replied.

"We appreciate how hard you work for us, Velora," he said, slinging the blanket over his shoulder and taking the basket. Then he wrapped his free arm around my back to my hip and tugged me to his side. "But don't forget you have a life, too."

"Of course." She dropped her glare to her work as he turned to face her.

"Come on, Audrey. I want to show you something. Oh, and speaking of life..." He led me out of the kitchen's back door into the herb garden and the bright, hot summer sunshine. "I want to take you to the summer festival. You'll love it, there'll be food and games and dancing."

As we turned to head deeper into the garden, I couldn't help but glance back into the kitchen. Nova flashed me a warm smile then turned her attention to inside the fridge, while Velora raised her gaze and returned to glaring at me.

The look sent a shiver of fear sliding down my spine. Shae, Sterling's girlfriend had worn a similar look when she thought that me moving in with Sterling and Merrick meant I was going to steal him from her.

Velora also hadn't been overly kind to me the night I'd arrived in Stonehaven and had dinner with Bishop, Cyrus, and their betas. I'd thought her dislike was because I was a weak shifter who was clearly keeping secrets along with me not being able to control my desire for Bishop and filling the room with the scent of my arousal.

Now I wasn't so sure.

Now it felt like she was angry Bishop was spending

time with me and not on a professional, they needed to get work done, level.

I could guess with the way Bishop unconsciously flirted and the looks other women gave him that he had a trail of broken hearts in his wake. What I didn't know was if Velora was one of them or was still hoping to catch his eye.

And really, who wouldn't want Bishop's attention? He was kind and funny and gorgeous. He was also a powerful catch. Anyone who mated with Bishop got as close to being a pack alpha as they could get. A woman could only get closer if she mated Cyrus, the primary alpha. But with his hurtful gruffness, he wasn't as desirable a catch as Bishop, no matter how bad-boy beautiful Cyrus was.

Velora probably wanted a rise in position in the pack along with the most eligible bachelor between the three brothers. But as far as I could see, Bishop hadn't shown any interest in her. Not at the dinner and not from the glimpse I'd just seen of them working together before he'd known I was in the kitchen.

And now I'd made an enemy of Velora.

She wasn't going to be able to obviously hurt or shame me like Shae and Sterling had done unless she got Cyrus's support which I doubted Knox or Bishop would allow. But that didn't mean she wouldn't try more subtle attacks.

I was going to have to be careful, especially when I was alone.

I'd already known I needed to watch myself and stay in my place until I'd quietly proven my usefulness, but this was more than that. Velora wouldn't be waiting for me to screw up, she'd attack regardless and when I least expected it.

BISHOP

"Lots of foreign merchants come to the festival and there's a ton of strange and interesting things to buy and eat," I said as I took Audrey's hand in mine and led her around the back of the Residence. I was excited to not just show her my favorite spot on the grounds but at the prospect of showing her the year's best festival. "It starts in six days, *after* you're done resting for Nova. Say yes."

She'd said she wanted all the things that came with courting, and that said to me that she wanted someone to make her feel special and desired. What was more special than a picnic in the gardens and a day dancing and laughing and eating and playing games at a festival?

She deserved all of it and more. It made me furious that no one had ever made her feel that way. And while Knox — once he got his head out of his ass — would be a dedicated mate and would protect her from everyone and everything, he wouldn't know how to make her feel like she was special. That was going to be my job and I was happy to do it.

Even if Knox came to me for advice — which he would when he realized the truth about our mate and that he had no idea how to give her what she deserved — I'd still be the mate to spoil her and treat her like a true alpha queen.

Because that was my job. I could protect her but not as well as Knox. I might be able to challenge her, but again, Cyrus was better than me at that.

Of course, first I had to get Cyrus to accept he had feelings for her. Which had been obvious even before he'd panicked over her being coerced by a magical connection and hurting herself. But he was determined to do right by our pack like our parents had taught him, and very few people in our pack would accept Audrey as an alpha.

They'd accept her as mine and Knox's mate, but not the mate of the primary alpha. At least not until they got to know her and realized her power didn't come from aggression and alpha strength, but determination and kindness.

With what she'd gone through, she could have been angry and hateful toward alphas and other shifters. She could have turned her determination into figuring out how to burn down the world — and I had no doubt she'd figure it out if she put her mind to it. Instead, she was soft and shy and tried to protect those who couldn't protect themselves to the detriment of her own safety despite her lack of power.

I squeezed her hand and glanced at her, and she responded with a soft warm smile.

"Say yes," I said.

Her warm smile faltered. I could see her insecurities starting to take over, insecurities that had only gotten worse since her heat fever and that monster's influence on her emotions.

Even with Whil's magic blocking him, the emotional wounds he'd insidiously inflicted on her heart and soul were still there, and it was going to take time for them to heal. It made me furious and broke my heart at the same time.

Audrey deserved to feel free to be herself, to do what she wanted without fear of anything.

But that confidence didn't happen right away, not with a lifetime of being abused. Going out, having fun, and seeing that my pack wasn't like her old pack would help. Everyone would be curious about her, the woman who mated Knox, but by going out they'd see she was perfect for us and fall in love with her, just like I had.

I fluttered my eyelashes at her and offered her my most innocent smile, drawing out her smile again with my goofiness. "Say you'll go to the festival with me."

She giggled and rolled her eyes. I could still see some hesitation in her expression, but I could also see her battling her insecurities. She *wanted* to go to the festival, to have fun.

"We'll have so much fun..." I batted my eyelashes again and added my flashiest smile, making her laugh.

"How can I say no to that?"

"So you'll go?" I asked.

"Of course I'll go," she laughed. "Now, where are you taking me for this picnic?" she asked as I led her past the small orchard with various fruit trees toward a towering hedgerow.

"To the prettiest place on the Residence's ground this time of year!"

"To Whil's greenhouse library?" Her lips quirked up at the edges and a hint of a mischievous glint danced in her eyes, telling me she'd already figured out we weren't anywhere near Whil's cottage.

"Nope. Prettier *and* more private." I waggled my eyebrows at her, happy to play her game, and was rewarded with a soft, musical giggle, one I wanted to spend the rest of my life hearing.

"What could be prettier than the gardens outside Whil's house? I bet those flowers bloom all year long despite the season."

"It's a side effect of her being summer fae," I said, leading her through a wrought iron archway set in the hedgerow and into the partially dead, partially evergreen winter garden. "She says unconsciously feeding the plants with a small but steady stream of magic isn't common among her people but does happen sometimes."

"She can't stop it?" Audrey asked, her gaze sliding

over the flowerbeds that would be vibrant and alive in winter.

"She can't. At least it doesn't drain her and just happens."

"I'm guessing it's only in a close vicinity to where she lives," she added. "Or these plants would be a lot happier."

"This is the winter garden. There's an assortment of evergreens and plants that flourish in the colder weather," I told her. "It's stunning with a light blanket of snow."

"But not where we're picnicking?"

"Nope. We're going to the summer garden... because it's summer," I replied taking her through another wrought iron arch in the hedgerow on the far side of the garden.

"Of course we are," she laughed then abruptly sucked in a sharp breath as she took in the summer garden.

Everything was in bloom in a cacophony of colors, shapes, and sizes. Purple, pink, and red clematises as well as purple wisteria and yellow honeysuckle climbed over the connected archways in the middle, creating a shady oasis where I was going to lay out the blanket for our picnic. I knew from all the hours I'd spent in my mother's garden that the grass was soft and the hush of the wind through the vines relaxing.

Surrounding the flower-covered shelter were rose bushes, daylilies, and daisies of various colors. There were also flowering shrubs covered in flowers, some big, others small as well as hibiscus, fragrant lavender, and dozens of other types of flowers.

"You're right," she said her eyes wide with wonder. "This place is stunning."

"The season gardens were my mother's passion when she could spare time from leading the pack. Our head groundskeeper and I have been keeping them blooming in her memory even though only a few of the Residence's residents come here."

"Why wouldn't they come?" she asked as I walked her to the vine-covered arches and laid out the blanket. "It's amazing here and so peaceful."

"A lot of people are busy." I urged her to sit and started setting up our picnic, beginning with the bite-sized appetizers and the wine.

This morning I'd begged Eloise, our cook, to put a romantic picnic together for me with the hopes that Audrey would be feeling better and wouldn't mind taking a short walk. Eloise had been more than happy to do it once she learned it was for the shy woman who'd been seriously hurt yesterday.

Apparently, the kitchen staff had noticed Audrey during the two nights she'd stayed with us and decided they liked her. She was quiet but very polite and gracious when they'd served her. A lot of strangers — like the foreign dignitaries who visited along with some of our pack members — looked down on them because they'd chosen to be of service to the alpha. But they weren't lesser than anyone else. We paid them a good wage and treated them with respect.

Audrey had lived through the same disparaging looks and remarks and had been looked down on, too, and I couldn't help wondering if the kitchen staff had seen a kindred spirit in her.

Regardless, they were going to be shocked when they learned that she'd mated Knox. Everyone would be shocked. But everyone would also know soon since Knox had lost his mind when she'd been hurt and hadn't cared who'd seen him or who he'd influenced with his power. And I had no doubt word was already racing through the pack about them.

That said, the kitchen staff were also going to be thrilled about Audrey and Knox mating because it meant she was staying.

"Wow, you're really going all out on this picnic," she said as I handed her a glass of wine. "*Hors d'oeuvres and* wine and it's only just after lunch."

"What does the time of day have to do with anything?" I frowned. "And what's an *hors d'oeuvres?*"

She pointed to the mini appetizers. "That's an *hors d'oeuvres*. Guess the magical translator stuck in my head doesn't translate French."

"That's another language in your realm? But not one you're fluent in?"

"Yeah." She sipped at her wine, her expression thoughtful. "I wonder how this translator actually works. It didn't translate TV or movie because you don't have those things in your realm. But it also didn't translate *hors d'oeuvres*. Which is a word that didn't originate in my native language but is still in common use. Most people in my realm who speak my language probably know what the word means."

"So that means it's common for people from different cultures to communicate with each other?" It was the only reason a word from a foreign language could become common use.

The thought astounded me. We had messengers and so did the neighboring packs, kingdoms, and city states, but it took days, sometimes weeks or even months to reach them.

A dialogue between our pack and other communities, especially those we didn't share a language with was slow and infrequent. There were only a few people in the pack who'd learned a second language and no part of those languages had become common use in ours, especially if we had our own word for it.

"My realm has more technology than yours," she said. "I've told you about TV, movies, and photography. We've also discovered the telephone, which, now that we've set up a whole bunch of wires, lets us talk with anyone around the world. Close to the time we discovered the telephone, we also discovered radio waves which can be used to communicate with someone within the waves' radius..." She frowned and sighed, the look so adorable I wanted to kiss the little wrinkles in her forehead.

"I can't remember how big it is," she said after some

thought. "But it doesn't require wires. Then we made cell phones which are phones that connect to a tower without wires, kind of like a radio but I'm not sure if they use radio waves or some other kind of wave. That wave connects with towers that relay the signal and sometimes relay that signal to a satellite in space so you can reach someone on the other side of the planet. Oh, and then we have the internet which is a bunch of computers that people can connect to with their own computer. Through that, we can talk to anyone anywhere with email or in chat rooms."

I took a big gulp of my wine, thrilled that the tension she'd had when she'd stepped into the kitchen was relaxing, but also overwhelmed with everything she said. There was so much information in that little speech, most of which I didn't understand, and the idea of communicating with someone anywhere in an instant was astounding.

Audrey sighed, her expression turning sad. "I thought maybe I could work with the pack's scientists and engineers and share what I have in my realm, but I don't know how any of it works. I just know what it does."

"But you know *of* these things," I assured her, squeezing her hand and hoping to bring back her smile. "Even if we can't make all of it, we might be able to make some of it. Hell, even if we can't make any of it, I love hearing about it. Your realm sounds incredible."

A shadow of fear swept over her expression.

Shit. Not what I wanted to do.

"Not all of my realm is great," she said, her voice too soft.

"Not all of my realm is great, either, but there are some incredible things within it, like our healing elixir, this garden, and—" I pulled Audrey into my lap and hugged her. "— you. You're incredible."

"Bishop," she admonished, her cheeks turning pink, but she didn't try to push out of my hold. Instead, she leaned into it, pressing her nose against my neck and drawing in a deep breath of my scent.

"Your idea is a good one," he said. "Once you're no longer restricted to the Residence's grounds, I'll arrange a meeting with our chief scientist, chief engineer, and Whil since she might know of something magical that would help with your new inventions."

"Well, they're not *my* inventions," she murmured against my neck.

"In this realm, they will be." I pressed my lips to the top of her head. Sisters, she smelled so good. I could hold her and be wrapped in her scent forever. In fact, I wanted to.

But I needed to take it slow, prove to her that I was in love with her not because her bond with Knox was influencing me — which it wasn't — but because she was everything I wanted in a mate and so much more.

"Our history books will tell the story of a brave young woman who brought the ideas for our technological advancement. And," I added, a new realization flashing through my mind. "You'll bring economic prosperity, too.

We'll have things no one else will have. We could sell them to get more water for our elixirs instead of sending hunters to work for our allies. We could also sell them to get more of that sedative Kelna makes. Nova hasn't stopped talking about it since we showed it to her. We could also—"

"Alright," Audrey giggled, grinning at my enthusiasm. "I get the point. I'm not as useless as I thought I was. I know things no one else does."

"And there's more to you than just that." I hooked my thumb under her chin and urged her to look at me.

She turned her brown eyes, almost gold in the streams of brilliant sunlight cutting through our leafy canopy, and mesmerized me, stealing my breath. She was so beautiful, so fragile, yet also incredibly strong. I'd do anything to make her mine, to convince her she belonged in this pack with me and Knox.

"You'll find your place in this pack and people will see you as I see you. Kind, compassionate, gorgeous, and strong," I said.

She opened her mouth to protest, but I brushed my lips against hers, silencing her.

"There's more to strength than physical prowess, alpha power, or being a good fighter," I whispered against her mouth. "You've been afraid and confused and heart-broken, yet you've risked your life to protect those who couldn't protect themselves. You've been beaten down, but you always, quietly get back up. You don't give up and you don't make a big deal about it. You just do it. If you decide something needs to be done, especially if it involves children, I have no doubt it'll get done."

"I don't want any child to go through what I went through."

"And on your watch, it'll never happen. You're incredible." I brushed my lips against hers again, aiming for another soft, sweet kiss, but she tangled her fingers in my hair, held me close, and deepened our kiss.

My wolf howled in pleasure, and I could feel, at the very edge of my consciousness, Knox's wolf howling back. This was where I belonged, where *we* belonged, loving this incredible woman and helping her to see in herself what we saw.

AUDREY

I KISSED BISHOP WITH EVERYTHING I HAD, TRYING TO match the passion in his eyes, while desperately wanting to believe his words. I wanted to be as strong as he said I was, but I couldn't even pretend he was right. I never stood up for myself, it was always too dangerous, and that made me a coward.

Even now I wasn't willing to stand up to Cyrus. It was always best to be as unnoticed as possible.

And while I had fought those two grimalkins, both times it had been a fluke, an impulsive decision and a bad one at that. I hadn't thought it through, just reacted, just like I'd reacted when Knox's wolf had taken control of his body and refused to let go. I might have been exhausted and vulnerable and partially manipulated by Sterling at the time, but that didn't make what Cyrus said to me any less true.

Bishop cupped the back of my head and returned my

passion, his tongue raking against mine, his breath picking up like mine.

Heat gathered low within me and the desire I'd always had for Bishop electrified my nerves, proving that my yearning for him had never been my heat. He made my soul sing with his kindness, compassion, and warmth. His stunning face and sleek muscles didn't hurt, either.

I brushed my hands down his shirt then dipped under it, tracing the hard lines of his abs with my fingers and drawing a soft moan.

"So we're playing dirty," he said, his voice deliciously gruff.

"This is dirty?" I trailed my fingers higher, sliding them along the bottom ridge of his pecs.

"You know it is," he groaned. "Now all I want to do is touch you back."

"So why don't you?" I purred, hoping and praying he'd touch me like I was touching him... except lower.

"Because groping isn't something a person does on a first date."

"I'm pretty sure we're beyond first date rules. We've already had sex." Fire burned my cheeks at the memory of my heat... or at least the erotic flashes that I could remember. "A lot of sex that I don't really remember."

"Heats don't count and I promised I'd court you. That starts with dates and perhaps a little kissing."

"That's how it works, hunh?" I raised an eyebrow and gave him my driest look. I didn't just want kisses, I wanted more, I wanted what we'd had our first night together in

Kelna, and I didn't want to wait any longer. "Those are *your* rules. There's nothing that says I can't grope you."

I swept my hands up his chest to his collar bone then slowly dragged my nails down his skin to the waistband of his pants.

Bishop groaned but didn't pull my hands away. "Audrey, you're killing me."

"You should probably do something about that," I said, my voice husky. I didn't know where this flirtatious woman had come from or how I was so confident in this moment, but I liked it. For just a moment, I felt powerful, able to bring this incredible alpha in front of me to his knees with desire.

With a growl, he captured my lips again in a searing kiss that stole my breath, a kiss that was more like my dream-Knox than the Bishop I knew.

His tongue plundered my mouth and his hand in my hair tightened, controlling my head, while his other hand pushed under my shirt and swept a blazing line to my breast.

Moaning, I arched into his touch, urging him for more. For everything.

But he broke off the kiss, his breath heaving, expanding his broad chest with every quick inhalation. Then he grabbed the bottom of my shirt, pulled it up over my head, and tossed it to the far side of the blanket. His heated gaze raked over my skin, starting at my waist, rising to my breasts, and stopping at my face.

The desire in his eyes tightened my core and made

my blush burn hotter, sweeping down my neck to the top of my chest. I dropped my gaze to the ground, unable to meet that intensity and maintain eye contact.

Except that was a mistake and I now had a perfect view of his thick erection straining the front of his pants.

"You're so beautiful," he breathed, making me suddenly self-conscious.

I wasn't beautiful. I had too many horrible scars.

I crossed my arms over my chest, but it was a futile attempt. I couldn't cover my nudity and all my scars at the same time. There were just too many of them.

"None of that," he said as he brushed his lips over the new scar at the top of my left breast. It sat right over my heart and the whisper of his touch sent desire shivering down my spine. "I think you're gorgeous and I intend to convince you that I'm worthy to be your mate."

"You are worthy." He'd always been worthy from the moment we'd first met and he was kind to me when he'd made my first time having sex wonderous and beautiful. I was the one who wasn't worthy.

"I'm still going to court you. This is the first of many dates. I want to show you all the best places and all the best people in Stonehaven. I want to watch sunsets and sunrises with you that don't involve hiking across the countryside all day. And I'm definitely taking you dancing. At the festival and afterwards." He punctuated each item on his list with a gentle kiss, inching lower and lower until his nose nuzzled against my arm covering my nipple, begging for access.

I hesitated a moment. Did I really want to do this? Only a few seconds ago, I'd thought I did, but we were still outside, and despite Bishop saying no one visited this garden, someone could still see us.

Of course, I'd probably been more out in the open when Knox had gone down on me last night and that hadn't bothered me, but I'd also been caught in mine and Knox's emotions. I wanted our mating to work so badly, I couldn't have said no if I tried.

This time, I didn't have another set of emotions urging me on and I *still* wanted him. I wanted the confirmation that he wanted me — even though logically I knew he did and wasn't lying.

"It's not fair if I'm the only one naked," I murmured, a small spike of fear stabbing through my chest at my bold words.

"You're still wearing pants," he said, his lips brushing over my skin, sending hot need racing to my core. "You're not naked."

"But I will be," I moaned, my voice breathy with desire.

"Your wish is my command." He slid me off his lap then yanked his shirt and pants off and settled back on the blanket beside me.

I stared at him, stunned at how quickly he shed his clothes, but also at all his mouthwatering muscles — along with his already thick cock, fully engorged and standing at attention.

With a grin that told me he knew he'd stunned me —

I was probably drooling, too — he leaned forward and kissed me.

The kiss was tentative at first as if he were afraid that stripping naked was too much for me. But when I didn't pull away and teased my tongue against his lips, he opened with a low, delicious growl and wrapped his arms around me, pulling me back onto his lap.

Desire coursed through my system, reigniting my yearning and pooling hot between my thighs. All doubt about being naked out in the open was gone, all that mattered was the incredible man kissing me and hopefully about to do more.

I tangled my fingers in his hair, holding him close. I'd never get enough of Bishop's kisses or his body.

And yes, I recognized how weird that was since Knox and Bishop had the same body. But to me they were different, completely separate individuals. I didn't see them as two versions of the same person. Bishop was Bishop and Knox was Knox. Both attractive in their own way.

Bishop kissed me until I was breathless and squirming. Then he set me back on the blanket, kissed his way down to my breasts, and ran his tongue slowly, oh so slowly, over my nipple.

I moaned, the heat within me surging, and he repeated the sensual lick then sucked the tight bud into his mouth.

"Bishop," I gasped as my back arched, pressing my breasts closer to him.

He pulled off with a pop, flashing me another wicked smile, and turned to my other breast, giving it the same agonizingly slow lick.

I tightened my grip on him and held him close, letting the pleasure rush through me and spin me tighter.

"Fuck, Audrey. I want you so much," he groaned against my breast.

"Then have me." I lay back, more confident than I'd ever been in my whole life, and propped myself on my elbows to maintain eye contact. "Please."

AUDREY

I LET MY GAZE, FILLED WITH NEED, SLIDE DOWN BISHOP'S body to his cock. He was so hard for me the head was an angry red, and thick veins stood out along his length. Precum already glistened at his slit, and as I watched, a drop broke free and trailed down, disappearing into the thick hair at his base.

I licked my lips, unable to help myself, and brought my gaze back to his. His eyes widened for a split-second as if he were surprised at what he saw, then his pupils expanded and darkened, making the green fleck stand out.

With a growl that heightened the desire racing through me, he surged forward and kissed me again. This time the kiss was wild, his tongue tangling with mine, his hands finding my breasts and kneading them. No more soft sweet kisses. This was Bishop unraveling, sinking into his need for me.

My breath picked up and he kissed his way back to my breasts, sucking on each nipple before going lower. He licked around my belly button and teased the skin just about the waistband of my pants, making me tremble, desire swirling like lava through my veins and pooling low.

"These have to go," he growled at my pants.

"Yes," I agreed breathlessly. "Please."

He quickly undid the tie that held the fabric up, hooked his fingers in the waistband, and pulled them down. Somehow, he regained some control and drew them down so... damned... slowly that I was panting with anticipation before he'd gotten them to my ankles.

Once they'd joined my shirt on the other side of the blanket, Bishop slid his hands up the insides of my thighs, and I let them fall open in invitation.

His eyes darkened even more, his wolf rising close to the surface, and he drew in a deep breath then hummed it out in pleasure.

"One taste is never enough," he said, replacing his hands with his lips and kissing higher and higher up my thigh.

"I'm pretty sure you've tasted me more than once," I replied with a shiver, my breath turning short and sharp. I had disjointed flashes of him going down on me during my heat, but nothing was clear.

"Heat fevers don't count." He blew a warm breath over my folds, the sensation adding to the building heat in my core. But he didn't put his lips where I wanted them and kissed down my other thigh to my knee. "Fevers are medical emergencies. The sex was necessary, not romantic. This..." he purred, kissing his way back up to my core. "This is romantic."

He blew another warm breath over me then flicked his tongue out. It was just a quick touch, not even close to my clit, but sensation jolted through me and my breath hitched.

"You taste so good. So sweet and perfect," he groaned before sliding his tongue through my folds with a slow, sensual lick. "So much like home."

My breath caught again and I dug my fingers into the blanket, needing to hold on to something, but not sure what.

Bishop ran his tongue over me again and again, building up my desire without even touching my clit.

Oh, please. Oh, please please please.

But he avoided touching that sensitive nub, spiraling my need so tight that I was gasping and moaning and not caring if someone could hear us. My desire had grown into an inferno and I couldn't catch my breath. The ache in my core told me I was close, so close, and yet not close enough. If he'd just touch my clit.

"More," I gasped, bucking into him, my whole body trembling. "Please, more."

He grabbed my hips, holding me still, and pressed closer, raking his tongue inside me and nuzzling my clit with his nose with the lightest of touches. Despite that, I still jerked against his grasp.

Oh, yes!

I just needed a little more pressure on that sizzling bundle of nerves. I was sure that was all I needed to go tumbling over the edge.

Bishop rumbled in pleasure, the sound vibrating from my core and up through my body.

Oh, please, I mentally chanted. *Please please please.*

Then he sucked hard in my clit and stars exploded behind my lids.

"Oh, yes!" I cried as pleasure rushed through me, stealing my breath.

"That's my girl," Bishop purred, licking at my release for a moment before crawling up my body and capturing my lips in a searing kiss.

His cock nudged at my entrance and before I'd fully come down, I was rocking up into him, brushing my sensitive, soaked folds against his tip.

"You're so beautiful with your hair wild and your face and chest flushed."

He pressed his cock at my entrance and slowly pushed inside, giving me lots of time to adjust to his girth. But I was so wet and relaxed from my orgasm that there wasn't even a whisper of pain, just the glorious feeling of being full and having every nerve in my channel bursting back to life.

We were both panting by the time he'd pushed all the way in and my walls were already fluttering, ready for another release. Then he started moving, slowly sliding out and pushing back in, rebuilding the needy ache inside me, and my thoughts scattered.

My body matched his rhythm, rocking my hips and urging him deeper as more bliss built inside me. The feel of him sliding in and out and raking against already sensitive flesh, while his body bumped my clit over and over again soon had me spinning. My pleasure wound tight and hot in my core and my breath turned ragged.

Bishop picked up his pace, soft grunts and growls escaping his lips, as his eyes darkened. They were almost fully black with only a few specks of green remaining, and that meant I was no longer just making love to Bishop.

His wolf had risen high enough to take over. So far, I didn't think he had, but it wouldn't have bothered me. His wolf was a part of him and it was natural for the more primal part of a shifter's soul to join or take over during moments of passion.

His rhythm started to falter, his hips working faster and faster, his thrusts snapping harder and harder into me. I moaned, my pleasure still building, an electric tingle at the base of my spine that was almost there, almost to the edge of an earth-shattering release, but not quite.

Once again, I was so close, and while it was selfish to want another one when Bishop hadn't had any, I couldn't help myself. The pressure and ache and the electricity racing through my veins felt so good. I didn't think I'd ever get enough of how Bishop made me feel.

In his eyes, I was beautiful despite my scars, and I was safe. I knew in my heart he'd always be there for me, and even though I ached for another orgasm, I also wanted this moment to last forever.

"Fuck, Audrey," he growled as he roughly rubbed his thumb against my clit.

Sparks burst through my body and the pressure inside me exploded. Every muscle in my body contracted, and a scream was ripped from my lips. More stars flooded the darkness behind my lids, brighter and sharper than before, and I spun around and around, gasping and shivering as the sensation overwhelmed me.

Bishop groaned his release, his body locked inside me as all his muscles contracted, too, and we held each other, spinning on brilliant, bone-melting bliss.

Then after a long moment of gasping for breath, he pulled out, and we resettled, lying on the blanket with me in his arms, my back to his chest.

"That was not how I expected our picnic to go," he said, sounding dazed and sleepy. "It was so much better."

He grabbed his shirt and helped me into it, warming my heart with his consideration for my discomfort at being naked in public, then wrapped me in his arms again.

The sound of his heartbeat and the warmth from his body, along with the summer heat and the sounds of insects and birds and the gentle breeze in the garden soon pulled me into a satisfied sleep.

When I woke, Bishop was gone. I was still in his shirt,

but Knox, in his wolf form lay beside me, sending a rush of uncertainty racing through me.

There was no way Knox didn't know I'd had sex with Bishop. I was covered in his scent and the scent of sex, was wearing his shirt with no pants, and — I bit back a groan — he would have felt us having sex through the mating bond.

He'd wanted me to also mate with Bishop... but did he really or had that just been when he hadn't been willing to work on our relationship?

AUDREY

THE SECOND I THOUGHT KNOX WOULD BE ANGRY WITH ME
for sleeping with Bishop, he woke and I was flooded with
contentment. Not even a flicker of anger or jealousy. He
really did want to share me with his brother, which was
so unlike the wolf shifters in my realm it made my head
spin.

Worry seeped into the bond and he nuzzled closer
to me.

What's wrong? he asked.

"Nothing," I replied, sitting up and tugging Bishop's
shirt down to ensure I wasn't flashing him or anyone who
walked by.

You're confused and worried. Did Bishop do something?
Did he hurt you?

"Did it feel like he hurt me?" I murmured, not
wanting to rub in the fact that Bishop and I had been inti-

mate again when Knox and I had only had intercourse once and I barely remembered it.

It felt like you wanted it and enjoyed it. But that doesn't mean you don't regret it now.

"I'd only regret it if it makes you angry at me and your brother. But it was just a silly thought." I pressed my hand over my heart. "I know it isn't true."

I already told you I wanted you to mate with him. He sounded genuinely confused about why I'd even think such a thing as well as a little hurt and those emotions radiated through our bond, making my insides squirm.

"It was just habit. Wolves in my realm are possessive of their mates," I told him. "And I know you told me you wanted me to mate with Bishop, but that was before you agreed to work on our relationship. I didn't even think that being with Bishop might upset you until I found you here, beside me."

You have nothing to worry about. Bishop and his wolf want you, and he'll be able to offer you things I can't, he said. *It's only an issue if you don't want him. But it sounds and feels like you do.*

My cheeks heated at the thought of what Bishop and I had done... outside... where anyone could have seen us. But even though I was embarrassed, I wouldn't have changed what we'd done. I'd loved every second of being with him.

Contentment from Knox radiated through our mating bond, igniting a spark of hope inside me. Maybe it would all work out.

I liked Bishop a lot and was relieved Knox wasn't going to demand we stop seeing each other. I could also feel my affection for Knox growing. He wasn't ignoring me, being terse or rude, or making demands like before. Maybe I was finally free. Maybe, so long as everyone else left me alone, I finally had a life with people who cared about me.

It smells like you didn't finish your picnic, Knox said, sniffing the basket.

"Barely even started." More heat bloomed across my face and I tried to get my blush under control. I had nothing to be embarrassed about. Bishop was going to be my mate, too. There was nothing wrong with having sex with him.

Then we should finish it. Knox's body turned to liquid, and in the blink of an eye, he'd shifted into his human form. "We wouldn't want all of Bishop's hard work to go to waste."

I gaped at him, unable to stop my gaze from sweeping over the contour of his chest and arms and down to his rippled abs and his partially erect cock.

The blush I'd been trying to control burned over my scalp and down my neck onto my chest.

"Could you—" I jerked my attention away, realizing even if I asked him to get dressed, he couldn't. He hadn't brought any clothes with him, and Bishop had taken his pants when he left.

Jeez. Nudity wasn't a thing with shifters, but I couldn't seem to get past it.

Of course, it didn't help that he was gorgeous.

And now I couldn't stop thinking about how amazing his mouth had felt when he made me come.

He grunted — but I couldn't feel any frustration in our bond — and grabbed my shirt on the other side of the blanket, using it to cover himself.

"Let's see what Bishop left us," he said, not addressing what most shifters thought was a ridiculous reaction to being naked.

He tugged the basket closer and pushed aside the cloth that was protecting the food. "Mini appetizers, three different types of sandwiches, two with wild mountain blackbuck cheese, sweet red berries, and two types of confection." A thread of worry seeped into the bond. "I should have thought of this."

"I feel like this isn't your thing," I told him, trying to send my burgeoning love for him through our bond.

"But it makes you happy."

"And I'll be happy with whatever you think will be an enjoyable date. You're your own person. You don't have to do what Bishop does. That, and I get the feeling that Bishop has had a lot of experience with this kind of thing." I gave him a wry smile and picked up one of the four remaining *hors d'oeuvres* and offered it to him. "I wouldn't have thought of it, either."

With a tentative smile, he took it and popped it into his mouth, his pleasure at what he tasted flowing through our bond.

Over the next couple of hours, we finished off Bishop's romantic picnic and chatted... which turned out to be a little awkward since I wasn't very good at casual conversation and Knox was terrible.

Still, it made me feel special to have Knox open up a bit to me. I suspected there were very few people he'd have an hour-long conversation with, let alone two hours — even in an enormous, open field. I could feel in our bond that he genuinely wanted to talk with me and that he was trying to make an effort, as promised.

"We should do something tomorrow," I suggested as I pulled on my pants. The more time we spent together, the more we'd figure out our relationship.

But Knox frowned in the middle of packing everything back into the basket as if he hadn't expected me to propose another date, and uncertainty rushed through our bond.

My own uncertainty rose to meet his. Had I been too bold? I'd thought we'd been getting along, but maybe that had all been in my head. Maybe Knox had been humoring me, which wasn't like him and I hadn't felt it in our bond, but I still couldn't shake the fear that I was wrong. Again.

Knox's eyes widened and his uncertainty switched to fear. "What are you thinking? What did I do wrong?"

I opened my mouth to tell him "nothing," but with our ability to sense each other's feelings he'd know right away I was lying.

"You don't want to see me again," I replied instead, fighting to keep my tone neutral even though I knew he could feel my churning emotions. "That's fine. I'm disappointed," I added because I definitely couldn't hide that from him, "but we can go at your pace."

"That isn't—" He pressed his hand over his heart, realization flooding his expression and our bond.

"We can't hide anything from each other," I said, saying what I knew he had to be thinking, "even if it's to protect the other's feelings."

"Fuck," he hissed, raising his gaze to meet mine. "I do want to do something with you tomorrow. Being with you is easy. Like being with my brothers, or Nova and Deacon."

"But..." I prompted. I could feel his sincerity and see it in his eyes. He did want to spend more time with me, but I could also feel the "but" hiding in the wings, waiting to come out.

"But I leave in a few hours on a hunt. That's why I'd originally come looking for you and found you asleep on Bishop." His gaze slid to the basket between us and a hint of shame curled through the bond. "I didn't want to reject your suggestion. I've done too much of that already. But I didn't know how to tell you I couldn't spend tomorrow with you."

I couldn't decide if I wanted to laugh or cry at the ridiculousness of the situation. I'd gotten so worried and he'd gotten upset because he didn't know how to decline a suggestion... probably without being brusque and rude like before.

Being able to sense each other's emotions was a

dangerous thing, especially since we still didn't fully trust each other.

"I have to work tomorrow, Audrey," I said, providing him with the appropriate response.

He frowned, confused. "That's it? You'd accept that?"

"You and Bishop have responsibilities to the pack. I hope I'll have some soon, too. Working or just needing a little space because this is too much peopling or because you've got some other engagement is a perfectly acceptable answer. I understand that you have a life and we don't know how I fit into it yet."

"But I promised I'd try." Worry colored his voice and rushed through our bond, breaking my heart for him. I wasn't sure exactly what had made him completely change his behavior with me, but it was obvious he wasn't used to it, just as it was obvious he meant what he said. He wanted to make our relationship work and I knew he wouldn't use his work as an excuse to avoid me.

"You can continue trying when you get back from the hunt," I told him. I cautiously reached for his hand and met his dark gaze. "I'll look forward to your return."

A tentative smile curled his lips, softening his usually hard expression, while relief and surprise filled our bond. "It'll only be four or five days."

I matched his smile. "Then I'll see you in four or five days. Which will be perfect because I'll be finished my doctor-mandated period of rest in four days."

Knox grunted, the happiness I'd felt when we'd been chatting returning. With his soft smile growing a little more, he finished loading the basket, handed me back my shirt, and shifted into his wolf.

I'll take this back to the kitchen, he said. *And I'll see you in four or five days.*

I opened my mouth to tell him that I had to return to the kitchen to figure out how to get back to my suite and I could take the basket with me, but he was already at the metal arch in the hedgerow, trotting with ease despite the basket handle in his teeth.

With a sigh, I laid back, propping myself up on my elbows, and looked up at the interwoven vines, their flowers a cacophony of color curling over the pergola. Soft beams of sunlight cut through foliage softly *shushing* in the breeze.

It was so peaceful here. Bishop had picked the perfect place for our picnic, and while I was a little sorry we didn't get to eat it together, I wasn't at all sorry for what we'd done instead.

A shiver teased down my spine with the memory of how good Bishop had made me feel, how loved. There was no doubt in my mind that Bishop was telling the truth when he said he was going to court me, and if this was the beginning, I couldn't wait for more.

I drew the collar of his shirt up to my nose and inhaled his fresh-cut grass scent, my smile deepening. God, I loved how he smelled. Crisp and bright and fresh. I could wrap myself in his scent forever and never get tired of it.

I could also wrap myself in Knox's deep, rich smoldering wood smoke scent. He was a warm, thick blanket and a hot chocolate on a winter's night, and despite our rocky start, I wanted to keep cuddling with him.

Things wouldn't be automatically easy between us, but today — and last night — had been a good start. Being able to feel his emotions also helped. I could tell he genuinely wanted to try to make our relationship work and that he felt guilty for how he'd treated me.

Of course, I still wasn't going to let him off easy.

As much as I knew how he felt, I wasn't ready to trust him with my body, not completely. I wanted to know him better, figure out how we could make a life for ourselves even if it wasn't the life either of us had wanted.

With that said, I was going to have to figure out how to be useful to the pack. Bishop had seemed excited about me sharing ideas from my world. If I was really going to do that, I needed to get my thoughts together and write down what I did know about things. Especially things that the pack might find useful. Which meant I needed a pen and some paper.

I sat up, considering who I might ask for them. I doubted I'd run into Knox before he left and Bishop could be anywhere. I certainly didn't want to go wandering about the Residence unescorted until I knew for sure if Cyrus would allow it.

Sure, Nova had suggested it, but she wasn't the alpha. She was someone else who might loan me writing stuff, but again, I didn't want to go hunting for her.

Maybe there was something in my suite. I hadn't

explored my new rooms since they'd been given to me...
yesterday evening...? The day before yesterday evening?
Yeah, I guess that had been the day before when we'd
gotten back from our trip north.

I'd been too tired and fidgety to check things out, then
I'd woken upset, had that catastrophic moment with
Knox and Cyrus, and Sterling had tried to get me to kill
myself. I hadn't even gotten a chance this morning when
Nova woke me and hurried me out to get food.

So, check the room first, then find the one person I
trusted or the other person I sort of trusted... or wait for
them to find me.

That was probably the safest option. If I just stayed
where I was, eventually one of them would come looking
for me.

With that decided, I glanced at my shirt, decided I
didn't want to take off Bishop's shirt, and headed back to
the kitchen so I could find my way back to my suite.

Thankfully, I didn't meet anyone on the way there,
and when I entered from the herb garden door, the two
women I'd seen working in the kitchen earlier — the
older woman and the woman about my age — offered me
big smiles and more food while telling me supper would
be in a couple of hours.

Despite declining, I still left the kitchen with a bowl
filled with grapes, a hunk of cheese the size of my fist, an
apple, and two large dinner rolls. It was almost as if they
were worried that I wasn't eating enough.

I supposed I'd lost weight during our trip and from

my unnaturally long heat, but I hadn't thought I looked
that bad. Of course, when I'd looked in the mirror this
morning, I hadn't been able to see past all my scars to
really pay attention to my figure.

Food in hand, I stepped into the hall, reminding
myself to stay small and quiet and not to make eye
contact and challenge anyone. If I just minded my own
business and went straight to my room, everything would
be fine.

Really.

My pulse picked up and I strained to slow it down.
This was the first time I'd been alone since I'd woken up
and it was hard to ignore my worries that I couldn't relax
and be myself.

I'd felt so safe with Bishop and even Nova and now I
felt exposed and vulnerable.

Still, I couldn't look afraid. I squared my shoulders,
raised my head, and plastered on the calmest, most
submissive expression I could. I needed to look like I
accepted my position as the lowest ranking member in
the pack and was happy about it. That's what alphas
wanted.

I was halfway across the grand foyer, the lights glit-
tering in the enormous crystal chandelier and peppering
the red carpet with mesmerizing rainbow flecks of light,
when one of the massive front doors opened.

Calm and accepting and unobtrusive.

Except I was in the center of the foyer and couldn't
duck out of the way as Cyrus stepped inside.

Shit.

I froze in place, pinned by Cyrus's stern glare and unable to escape to the shadows so he could forget about me. I wasn't ready to run into him yet and I certainly hadn't wanted to face him for the first time since he'd yelled at me while I was alone.

And even while my body trembled — much to my mind's frustration — afraid he'd reprimand me again or do worse, the image of my fantasy flooded my mind's eye. Cyrus naked, all his powerful muscles on display as he held me gently, carefully, and slowly pushed inside me.

"Audrey," he said, his voice gruff as stuttering waves of power rolled off him as if he was trying to hold it back but was too upset to manage it.

"Alpha," I said, dropping my gaze to the floor, my cheeks heating with an unwanted blush despite my nervousness.

"You're going to ruin your dinner with all that." The front door shut with a thud, a finality that echoed through the room.

I opened my mouth to explain I hadn't wanted the food but also hadn't wanted to disrespect members of his pack by declining twice, then I remembered that was an excuse.

No excuse was ever good enough.

"Yes, alpha."

"Audrey," he huffed and another wave of power, this one sharp and stronger, jerked my head up to look at him.

Damn it. I didn't want to look at him, didn't want another glimpse of his bad-boy beauty, large, muscled figure, and the hard look in his moss green eyes. But I couldn't help myself. Just like his brothers, seeing Cyrus stole my breath.

A little more than a day's worth of scruff covered his square jaw, and the shaved sides of his head were longer as well as if he hadn't had time to shave in a while. The rest of his brown hair was tied back in its usual thick braid that reached the nape of his neck and I couldn't see any of the golden highlights that shone bright in the sunlight.

Audrey, remember your place! I snapped at myself and quickly yanked my gaze to a spot on the door behind him.

"Dinner really is in a couple of hours. Do you remember your way to the dining hall or should I send someone?" he asked.

From his curt tone and choice of words, that hadn't been a request. It was an order.

I didn't think it was a trap to get me in front of his betas so he could reprimand me again. That didn't seem his style, but I was still going to have to watch myself. Just because he didn't plan it to be a trap, didn't mean it couldn't become one.

Small. Quiet. Invisible.

With luck, if I kept to myself and he didn't see me with Bishop, he and everyone else would forget about me... at least until I'd proven my worth.

"I can find my way, alpha," I replied, trying to keep my worry from my expression.

"Good."

He marched down the hall toward the kitchen and I hurried in the opposite direction, realizing that I had no idea when exactly dinner was since a couple of hours was still somewhat vague, or how to tell if a certain amount of time had passed.

CYRUS

I PACED MY OFFICE UNABLE TO CONCENTRATE ON MY WORK even though stacks of reports and requests covered most of my large wooden desk. I'd been trying to concentrate for two hours now and hadn't gotten a thing done.

Seeing Audrey in the foyer had been the first time I'd seen her conscious since I'd yelled at her yesterday morning and she'd retreated into her shell. She was even more withdrawn than she'd been when she'd first arrived and I knew it had nothing to do with being manipulated into hurting herself and everything to do with me.

The thought squeezed my chest, making it hard to breathe, and I clenched my jaw against howling out my frustration.

I had to stay in control. And in better control than when she'd dropped her gaze in the foyer. My frustration at her retreating into herself and my guilt for hurting her enough that someone could have influenced her into her hurting herself were just too strong, and I'd been unable to fully contain my power.

No one could know how I really felt about Audrey, how I desperately wanted to go with my wolf's instinct, to say to hell with pack responsibilities, and court her like Bishop was. My wolf was determined to have her and all but the responsible side of my human half agreed with him.

Except it wasn't possible. She couldn't be mine. I had to remember that.

Why couldn't I remember that? Why couldn't I stop thinking about her, about how she'd worked so hard during our trip north, how she made something in my chest warm when she was near or smiling or relaxed, and how much I'd needed to protect her when she'd been suffering through her heat?

I'd thought her hating me would kill those thoughts and help me stay detached, that it was for the best for us to keep our distance from each other. It probably still was the best way to go about it. But that didn't stop all the air from being sucked out of the foyer when I'd stepped inside and she'd looked at her feet.

The air hadn't returned when I'd accidentally let my power slip and forced her to look at me. Her eye contact had been so brief, I couldn't help wondering if it had really happened before it slid to somewhere past my shoulder.

And then — of course! — I had to be me. I

commented on the first thing I noticed, the bowl piled with fruit and bread.

Dinner really had been in two hours, but she hadn't needed to be reprimanded about it. Eloise had probably told her when dinner was when she'd handed Audrey the bowl of food.

Knowing our head cook, the grandmother had taken one look at Audrey, decided she was too skinny, and wouldn't take no for an answer. Without a doubt, Audrey hadn't been able to decline the food.

And with me playing the villain in order to not let my attraction to her take over and keep her away from unnecessary scrutiny, she didn't want to explain that to me.

A growl slipped past my clenched jaw, the sound low and dangerous, and I was grateful there wasn't anyone around to hear me.

She'd shut down when I'd lost my mind with fear and yelled at her. She hadn't reacted the way I'd expected but I'd have thought she'd have regrouped by now. She was so determined about everything, it drove me crazy seeing her so submissive.

I could only pray her submissiveness was only with me and not everyone in the pack.

She obviously wasn't that way with Bishop. I'd overheard him asking Eloise for a romantic picnic and it looked like it had worked. She was wearing Bishop's shirt and had his and — much to my surprise — Knox's scent coating her like a second skin.

That, at least, was promising, especially if she was accepting Knox... unless, of course, I'd scared her so much she'd lost all her fight and was giving in to Knox's demands.

No. That couldn't be true. She was so determined to make him grovel, and after having the shit scared out of him and nearly losing her, I knew my brother would do everything in his power to make her happy... even if he didn't understand it.

Even without a bond between us like Knox had with Bishop, I'd felt Knox's terror. Hell, everyone in a two-hundred-foot radius had felt it, and without a doubt, the whole pack knew Knox had mate bonded with Audrey.

That was another issue that I wasn't sure how to deal with. How much did I interfere in Audrey's life? If I showed her too much favoritism rumors would start.

I huffed a bitter laugh. Rumors had already started from the moment we brought her to Stonehaven. I'd thought everyone would have gotten bored of the idea of me and her during the month we were away, but no. People were still talking about how I'd stormed into Nova's office to get a dress for Audrey, and now that she was here to stay, people would keep talking.

Damn it. I didn't know how to fix this. And I *really* wanted to fix this.

But fixing social problems was Bishop's job, and I had to stay out of it and be patient or I'd make things worse.

I slammed my fist against my desk, pulling back at the last minute so I didn't break it. I used to be good at patience, but it was getting harder and harder to stay in control.

I'd been the one who'd weakened her mental defenses so that asshole could convince her to hurt herself, and *I'd* been the one to make her afraid of me.

Her being submissive was all my fault and I hated myself for it.

Someone touched my mind, asking permission to talk to me, and I mentally touched them back, letting them know they weren't interrupting.

I've notified Audrey that dinner will be ready in ten minutes, Eloise said.

Thank you, I replied, as I ran a nervous hand over my head and silently prayed, *Please, let her submissiveness just be with me. Please, don't let me have fucked this up for her.*

I'd asked Eloise to notify Audrey about dinner since I had no idea if anyone had pointed out the clock on the mantle over the fireplace or if she even knew how to read it. I'd tried to ask Bishop to get her, he'd been the most obvious choice and the least likely to startle her, but he'd had to leave the Residence's grounds, and while I'd been able to reach him, he didn't have the telepathic strength to reach Audrey.

I headed out, knowing I'd get to the dining room early, but I couldn't continue to pace in my office. I'd check in with Eloise to see how she and Kira were doing. Eloise had a new grandchild — number two — who'd been born a few weeks before we'd left for the death god's temple, and Kira was studying foreign cuisine with a visiting Dedearc chef who'd been invited to take over the fanciest restaurant in town until the fall.

Except as I rounded the corner and strode into the wider hall where some of our small public rooms were, I saw Audrey, and all the air vanished again, from the hall, my lungs, from everywhere.

She sat on a bench in an alcove, leaning into the corner where the shadows were the deepest. But they weren't enough to hide her. Even tucked away, someone standing at the right angle — like I was — would be able to see most of her.

It also didn't help her that she'd worn a dark green dress. From her nervous posture, I suspected she thought it would help her blend into the background, but all it did was contrast with her pale skin and her blond hair and drew my attention to her hazel eyes and soft pink lips as if they were the only sparks of color on her black and white canvas.

She looked even more fragile than she had in the foyer and certainly before I'd yelled at her, and I couldn't stop staring at her. My heart hurt looking at her.

The memory of pushing into her warm hot sheath, her body too weak and exhausted, swept through me. I'd needed so desperately to protect her then, just like I needed to now. Except I had no idea how to do that and keep my distance.

CYRUS

BECAUSE YOU CAN'T PROTECT HER AND KEEP YOUR DISTANCE AT the same time, my wolf growled at me, fighting to take over and go to Audrey.

I mentally tightened my grip on him, willing him to calm down. *I have to.*

She's ours.

She can't be, I growled back at him, startling Audrey who turned wide eyes toward me before jerking her gaze to her feet.

Shit.

"You're early," I said, my voice gruff despite my effort to act natural... which clearly didn't work because she tensed, making me realize that my words, once again, could be a reprimand. "Punctuality isn't a bad thing," I added.

"Yes, alpha."

I cringed at her response. Talking about punctuality

could be a reprimand as well or be interpreted that if she was ever late, I'd punished her.

Sisters! How the hell did Bishop talk to women? This was a quagmire just waiting to swallow me whole.

"Cyrus," Finn called from down the hall, saving me from having to figure out what to say while also frustrating me that I hadn't fixed the situation. "Have you had a chance to look at the new watch schedule?"

"Yes," I said, forcing myself to turn away from Audrey so I could lead my watch commander away from her and into the dining room. "I like the extra shifts you've added, but I think we need at least two more men at the market. We can't risk endangering our economy by not having enough protection."

"I'll need to recruit more watchmen," Finn replied, taking his usual seat at the table. "We're stretched thin already. Unless you can recall ten of them back from Ciliran or Lais."

I sagged into my seat at the head of the table and sighed. "I wish I could, but we'd need to renegotiate our treaty with them since we can't replace the watchmen with hunters."

"If we could just get the beast population back under control," Finn added.

"It's not like we're not trying," Deacon said as he strode into the room. "We've got a dozen hunters in the hospital with serious injuries and are stretched thin as well."

"We might be able to do something about that,"

Lucius added, and I leaped from my seat and drew him into a hug.

"Welcome back." I squeezed a little tighter and held on a little longer than proper but I didn't care. I'd been back for two days now and our schedules had kept us too busy to talk before now.

Lucius had been a beta for my parents since I was little and his presence always steadied me. He was the rational, experienced one between me, my brothers, and our betas, and while Thane, our chief of finance, was rational to the extreme, he lacked Lucius's empathy that allowed him to offer logical *and kind* options for difficult decisions.

I released him and he took his usual seat as Thane and Velora entered followed by Bishop and a pale Audrey wearing a soft, bland smile that didn't reach her eyes.

"The discussion was good at the Mountain and Sea Alliance emergency meeting. But we weren't able to finalize anything because it really is something you should weigh in on," Lucius said. "Speaker Jundar, King Gower, Representative Folmar, and Pimryl will be coming here in three weeks to continue talks, and they've reported that they're in talks with merchants who have new weapons that are effective against any beast, even grimalkins."

Deacon whistled as Audrey took Knox's usually empty seat beside me, offering me a too-polite nod of acknowledgment, and Bishop sat beside her.

"I'll believe there are weapons that strong when I see it," Deacon said.

"His Majesty King Gower says he's seen them in action and can attest to their power. We'll know more when everyone arrives." Lucius sat back down and turned his attention to Audrey. "I see there's someone new joining us tonight. I'm Lucius."

Audrey's gaze flickered to mine as if asking permission to speak, putting a slightly too-long pause in the conversation before Bishop said, "She's Audrey."

"Knox's mate," Velora added a little too cheerfully.

She'd been interested in Bishop since we'd been kids and had thought being promoted to beta had assured her a place at his side, but he'd never expressed or shown an interest in her. I couldn't tell if she was relieved Bishop wasn't mated to Audrey or concerned they were still sitting too close together just to be polite like the last time we'd all had supper together.

"So the rumors are true," Lucius said, confirming my suspicions that the pack was talking about Knox and Audrey.

Audrey nodded, her gaze still on Lucius's right ear and the soft smile that didn't reach her eyes firmly in place.

Eloise and Kira came out with salads, warm rolls, and bottles of wine, and Audrey quietly thanked them whenever they set something in front of her. But she was so withdrawn, Eloise's smile quickly turned to a frown and the Residence's cook shot me a worried look.

I couldn't have agreed with her more. This wasn't the Audrey who'd had dinner with us a month ago, and it wasn't even close to the woman I'd seen in the final few days of our journey.

"I want to know how it happened," Velora said once Eloise and Kira had left. "We all thought Knox would never mate."

Again Audrey's gaze flickered to mine, making me squirm in my seat even if it made sense to look for my permission this time. The question involved more than just her and I doubted she wanted to say anything that might upset me or Knox.

Except whatever she said would be fine. It was her life and her mating and she had the right to tell as much or as little of it as she wanted. Although if she spoke the whole truth, that would bring up a lot of questions that I wasn't sure she wanted to answer.

"I want to know about that as well," Thane said, filling his and Velora's wine glasses then handing the bottle to Deacon. "If we know what got Knox to mate with you, perhaps it could help us get him to open up with the rest of us."

"Or really just open up with anyone," Finn added. He'd idolized Knox almost as soon as he could walk and had been angry — perhaps still was — that Knox had shut out everyone except me, Bishop, Nova, and Deacon.

"Well?" Velora pressed, turning her full attention to Audrey. "Did you lure him in with your feminine wiles?"

"No, beta," Audrey replied, her voice soft and bland like her expression, and her gaze locked on the far wall.

Velora huffed. "It's got to be something."

"It's complicated," Bishop said, an edge in his tone that I was sure only I heard because we were brothers and I'd known him all his life.

"What does that mean?" Thane asked, a small line forming between his brows, the precursor to a frown. Out of all our betas, he was the most curious and also the most socially oblivious.

Audrey's eyes flashed to Bishop for a second, the movement so subtle I wasn't sure if anyone else noticed, and she gave a tight nod as if Bishop had said something to her telepathically. It was rude to have a mental conversation with someone while at the table, but I wasn't going to call her or Bishop out on it. She needed the reassurance only Bishop could give her... because she needed to stay angry with me.

Except she wasn't angry. She was afraid of me and everyone else, just like I'd feared.

"It's complicated because they're fated," Bishop said, answering for her. Then he took a bite of his salad as if that statement answered everything, even though we both knew it wouldn't, not for Thane and not for any of our other betas.

Deacon and Nova didn't react since they already knew the truth, and thankfully they didn't correct Bishop about how Knox and Audrey weren't really fated. Although maybe they were and we were too upset to see the truth. That would explain why her incomplete mating bond had latched on to him and not Bishop.

Thane, however, frowned in full, while Finn and Velora looked shocked.

"You mean *fated* fated?" Velora stammered. "That's impossible."

"I'd have to agree," Finn added. "True fated mates are a myth."

"Clearly, they're not. It's the only logical explanation for why sweet Audrey here is mated to the grumpiest member of our pack," Deacon said, rolling his eyes at Thane.

The hint of Deacon's usual mirth curled his lips but didn't reach his eyes. He was trying to lighten the situation but was just as worried as I was about how the others were reacting. They were supposed to welcome her warmly, just like they had for her first dinner, or feel compassion for her for being mate bonded to Knox. But instead, they were suspicious and that agitated my already agitated wolf even more.

Thane's frown deepened. I could practically see the wheels in his head turning as he tried to solve the mystery of why Audrey and Knox were mated. "The most recent mention of fated mates was three hundred years ago."

"That's the only one mentioned and we don't know how accurate it is," Velora said.

Nova ripped a piece off her roll and gave Velora her

driest, least impressed look. "Whil wrote the book you're talking about. Why don't we go ask her if she made it up."

"Doesn't mean Knox and Audrey are true fated mates," Velora shot back, unwilling to back down, surprising me. If Knox and Audrey were fated, that would mean there was a greater chance she could have Bishop... unless, of course, she believed the rumors that because Knox and Bishop were twins, they were going to share a mate.

Of course, anyone close to Bishop — which didn't include Velora — knew it wasn't just speculation. Bishop had been saying to me and a few select others that he felt he'd share a mate with his twin since he was a teenager.

Nova raised an eyebrow, shooting me a questioning look, and ate her piece of dinner roll.

Yeah, I'd seen it, too. Velora was far too interested in Bishop and therefore Audrey. And because they both lived in the Residence, Velora could make Audrey's life more difficult without anyone else knowing.

Well, without anyone but Knox knowing. That would inevitably end with Velora pushing Knox too far and the pack demanding Knox be banished because he was too dangerous. And while people would be understanding that Knox was defending his mate, everyone was still afraid he'd snap, turn feral, and start killing people.

If I'd thought when we'd first promoted Velora to beta that her crush on Bishop would have turned into a problem, I'd have picked someone else. It wouldn't have mattered how organized and efficient she was.

But once again, I'd misread a romantic situation.

"They're mated now so it doesn't matter if they're fated or not," Thane concluded. Then he turned his attention to Audrey, his eyes bright with curiosity. "I have so many questions for you, like how far away is your old pack? You weren't comfortable in our loose clothing. Does that mean your environment is colder, or do you feel the cold more than we do?" He turned to Nova. "We should run a study. I'd be interested to know if there are biological differences between us and if so, does that mean her pack didn't originate from the Original Pack?"

"And then you'll want to know her exact height and weight and when she had her last heat," Deacon mocked.

"Oh! Yes! That's good information, too," Thane replied, completely oblivious to the fact that Deacon was making fun of him, while Audrey shrank deeper into her chair, embarrassment and worry starting to dampen her bland smile and seep into her eyes.

"We're not hounding Audrey with questions," Bishop insisted, his arm moving closer to her, his hand, hidden by the table, likely on her thigh to reassure her and steady her soul.

"No," Finn said. "Thane has a point. We know nothing about her and she's mated into the pack's alpha unit. She could be dangerous."

CYRUS

Bishop growled at Finn's words and power slipped from Deacon's control.

"Audrey isn't dangerous," I said, fighting to keep my voice even, while the urge to tear into Finn for making such an accusation squeezed my insides. "And just because she's mated into the alpha unit doesn't make her an alpha."

Audrey flinched and my stomach churned, threatening to expel what little I'd eaten of dinner. I hadn't meant to remind her about what I'd yelled at her in the arena, but I needed to stop my betas' worry and accusations before it got out of hand.

I didn't know how the conversation had twisted into them thinking Audrey was dangerous, and while I could understand my watch commander being suspicious, I hadn't expected Velora to be so outwardly hostile.

I'd always encouraged our betas to question decisions

with logical arguments so Bishop and I could get different perspectives on a situation, but it was driving both me and my wolf crazy that they were questioning my judgment when it came to Audrey.

Out of the corner of my eye — my glare still on Finn — I watched Audrey raise a trembling fork to her mouth as if she were trying to hide her discomfort by eating. But the fluttering piece of lettuce at the end of the utensil only made her shaking more obvious and she quickly set her fork aside and clasped her hands on the table.

Sisters, I needed to protect her, hold her, reassure her.

But I couldn't. I had to keep my distance.

"She's not an alpha," Finn agreed, "you're right. But that doesn't mean she can't influence you. I mean look at Bishop. He's obviously taken with her and we all know how he feels about women in distress." Finn drained his wine and set the glass on the table to punctuate his words. "She won't tell us where she's from or anything else about herself. You found her in Darkweald after that wave of power and then our hunt team found that strange magic in Anakar. How do we know she's not connected to that? How do we know she's not a spy or whether she intends to hurt the pack? She's already made all three of you leave for a month."

My wolf heaved at Finn's accusations and how Velora was nodding in agreement and Thane was looking thoughtful, actually considering Finn's words.

Come on, Audrey, I mentally begged, struggling to keep

my thoughts to myself. *Tell him to fuck off. That it's none of his business. Prove you can stand your ground.*

Sisters, I wanted to tell them all to fuck off, but that wouldn't help the situation. Everything would get worse if they started thinking I was interested in Audrey, too. She needed to speak up and prove that she might be powerless but she was still a person and deserved respect. But gods, my wolf was on the verge of taking over. How dare they question her and talk about her as if she wasn't even in the room!

"She didn't make us leave for a month, Knox did," Bishop said, his posture growing tense. "We all know how he felt about mating. *He* didn't want a bond and Whil had found a spell that might have helped."

"But it didn't," Finn pressed.

"Maybe Audrey found a way to force the bond on him," Velora said, catching Deacon mid-sip.

He sprayed wine across his salad and roll, his expression shocked, while Bishop's eyes narrowed, and my wolf howled and heaved inside me.

"If she was going to force a bond on anyone, why the hell would she pick Knox?" Deacon sputtered.

"Because she's too stupid to know Knox isn't really a pack alpha," Velora shot back.

Her words hit like one of Knox's punches to my chest, shattering what little hold I had on my emotions and my wolf. No one called my mate stupid because she sure as hell wasn't stupid.

"Enough!" I roared, a blast of my power snapping through the room.

My betas sat up straighter and stared at me with wide eyes, while Audrey shook even harder and paled to the point I was afraid she was going to pass out.

She wasn't even bothering to keep up her meek, bland mask, and she probably thought I was angry with her even though this conversation and my loss of control was my betas' fault.

Fuck. Fuck fuck fuck.

"Audrey is a member of my family," I growled, my wolf rising to the surface but not taking over.

Somehow, he understood that if he took over, my betas would accuse me of desiring her and not thinking straight, but he still wanted to show my betas— hell, show everyone, that he agreed with me. Audrey was family. Audrey was mine. This wasn't just something my human half felt strongly about. All of me felt this.

"You *will* respect her." I glared at Velora, making her tense.

Then I slid my gaze over everyone else to let them know it wasn't just Velora I was pissed at. Finn swallowed hard while Thane bobbed his head in agreement and Deacon and Nova looked concerned. Lucius on the other hand tipped his head in acknowledgment, pride lighting his eyes. He agreed with me defending Audrey. Hell, he could probably tell what everyone was thinking — which was why we'd made him our diplomat — and knew

Audrey was exactly what she seemed: a lost scared young woman with too many scars on her body and soul.

"I'd still like to know more about her," Thane insisted, his curiosity undeterred by my growl and power slip, because of course, he didn't see hounding Audrey with questions as disrespectful. "We could learn more about what lies beyond our territory and that of our neighbors."

"Thane," Deacon hissed, loud enough for the whole table to hear, including Audrey with her practically human hearing. "Stop while you're ahead."

Thane frowned. "But I'm not ahead. I still don't know anything new."

My huntmaster groaned and looked skyward. "Sisters, help me!"

Thane looked even more confused and Deacon burst out laughing.

If I hadn't been so angry about my betas interrogating Audrey, I might have laughed at Thane being Thane, too.

"This isn't funny," Finn insisted. "We don't know her intentions. She just shows up one day and is fated for Knox? I find that suspicious."

"Pup," Deacon groaned. "Just because you dated out of the pack and she turned out to be a lying manipulative bitch, doesn't mean Audrey is."

"But—" Finn protested.

"Whil already confirmed when Audrey first arrived that she has no ill intent and that everything she told us is the truth," Bishop said, while Audrey continued to tremble and stare at her plate.

Please. I tried to will her to look up and challenge my betas. *Say something. Stand up for yourself. Show them what you showed me and my brothers while we were traveling. Show them what I see in you.*

But she didn't move, just took it like she'd been taught, which only made me angrier.

A growl rumbled in my chest again and more power slipped my control. "This conversation ended a minute ago. It will *not* continue and will *not* be heard again."

But that only made my three suspicious betas frown.

"She's from another realm," Bishop said with a huff of frustration. None of us had wanted to reveal that until Audrey was ready because we knew she'd be inundated with questions.

And sure enough, Finn and Thane opened their mouths, but Bishop raised a hand and glared, silencing them.

"Whil has confirmed this is also true. Which means Audrey has no ulterior motives towards our pack. She didn't even know we existed until we found her."

"Then she knows—" Thane started.

"No," Bishop snapped.

He wrapped a protective arm across Audrey's shoulders and drew her to his side, doing what I wanted to do but couldn't without creating a mutiny among my betas or without sending Audrey the wrong signals... or maybe the right ones that I couldn't accept.

The thought twisted around my heart and made my

wolf claw at my insides, and I struggled to remind myself that it was best if Audrey didn't like me.

"If or when Audrey feels comfortable talking to you about it, she will," Bishop added. "Until then, leave her alone."

He pushed out his chair, helped Audrey stand, and led her out of the dining room.

Well, that went well, Nova said, her mental voice dry as Velora and Finn shoved back their chairs and left and Thane looked confused.

"You understand why Cyrus told you to back off, don't you?" Lucius asked him.

"Because I can be overwhelming when I get excited?" our chief of finance replied, making it sound like a question instead of a statement.

Nova nodded. "We're all curious. We just need to remember that Audrey doesn't know us and we might make her nervous."

As if that hadn't been obvious from the beginning. But Thane was worse than Knox when it came to reading body language and hadn't clued in on her distress.

Thane nodded. I'm not sure if he understood exactly what Nova meant — I wasn't sure if he ever did — but he knew enough that if we told him someone was upset or scared, he'd wait until we'd told him they were better.

We ate our main course discussing what went on with the pack while we'd been gone, Lucius's observations about the members of the Mountain and Sea Alliance, and the upcoming summer festival until Thane left.

Then Deacon poured himself another glass of wine and sagged back in his chair. "What the fuck, Cyrus? I leave you alone with her in the arena for ten minutes after you assured me she'd be fine and somehow the woman who walked with us to patrol shed twelve a month ago is completely gone. Did you do that after she saved Knox from going feral, or was that a build up from your entire journey north? She's clearly afraid of you."

"She was afraid of everyone here except Bishop," Lucius stated. "She was even wary of Eloise and Kira."

"Which she wasn't before," Nova added, grabbing the wine bottle in front of Deacon.

I ran my hands down my face, wanting to scream with frustration while also wanting to find her, grab hold, and never let her go.

This was all my fault. If I'd just talked to her instead of yelled, everything would be fine and she might not have nearly killed herself, but—

"She almost died in the arena," I insisted as if that was a good excuse for me losing my temper.

"So you decided to put the fear of the alpha in her to stop her from doing something else?" Nova rolled her eyes at me. "Well it worked. She was even nervous around me this afternoon when I checked in on her. I think she's more afraid of everyone than when she first arrived."

"I know that," I growled. "I can't fix that."

"Sure you can. You go up to her and apologize." Deacon took a long sip of his wine, waiting for me to agree. "I know you can do it. I've seen you apologize before. I've even seen you do it after you became primary alpha."

"It's not that simple," I shot back, even though I knew it was exactly that simple.

"Audrey, I'm sorry." Deacon glanced at Lucius and Nova. "I believe that was three words?"

Nova nodded in agreement. "I believe so."

"I concur," Lucius added.

I groaned and glared at Lucius. "Not you, too?"

"But if we need someone to count," Nova continued, "we should ask Thane. He's the genius when it comes to numbers."

"Come on, guys," I begged. "You know it's not that simple. The pack can't think I have any interest in her. They'll be worse to her than Thane, Finn, and Velora were."

Nova quirked her eyebrow again. "That would suggest you're interested in her."

"It doesn't matter if I am. You know how the pack gossips." And it would be worse if they knew that I really did want her, too hell with her being too weak to shift or anything else. "The only people who can fix this are you and Bishop. I don't want to confuse her."

"Why would she be confused?" Deacon asked as realization flashed across Nova's expression.

"Her heat. You said it turned into a fever that went on for nine days. You had to have sex with her."

"And sex means something to her, even if she doesn't

remember," I said, mumbling the last part. "I crossed that line and now I have to put that line back."

"I'm pretty sure you have." Deacon downed the rest of his wine and shook his head at me. "You've built a whole chasm between you and she'll never look you in the eyes again."

Which was exactly what I'd wanted and made my chest so tight I could barely breathe.

AUDREY

I clung to Bishop, desperately holding onto him and the warmth of his soul steadying mine. He'd rushed me out of the dining room before I'd even known what had happened, brought me to my suite, sat on the couch, and cradled me in his arms.

"You don't have to do that again. Ever," he said. "If I could, I'd demote them for scaring you."

"They don't know me and are trying to protect you and the pack," I forced out.

I didn't want to defend them, but I also didn't want to make them any angrier with me than they already were. And from the look on Velora's face, she was already furious and I suspected it'd be easy for her to convince Finn that I couldn't be trusted.

Thane on the other hand just seemed obsessively curious. I didn't even think he knew what he and the others were saying was scaring me, and God, did it scare me.

They talked about me as if I wasn't there, something Merrick did all the time, and just like my old alpha and his betas, they could do whatever they wanted to me. They could turn me into a test subject, lock me up forever, or turn the pack against me, just like Sterling had done with all the other kids in my old pack.

I'd thought I could just sit there and keep my expression neutral, but I should have known they wouldn't have ignored me, not with the look Velora had given me earlier when I'd left the kitchen to have lunch with Bishop.

And while Cyrus had defended me and told his betas that I was family, I had no doubt some of his anger was still directed at me. It was my fault they didn't listen to him and hounded me. If I hadn't been there, they would have had a perfectly normal conversation, and that had made me even more nervous.

This was his house and his pack. He couldn't let such disobedience go without punishment and without a doubt, that would mean punishing me for making his betas question him.

The punishment might not happen right away because I was currently with Bishop, but I doubted Cyrus would forget about what had happened. He'd made how he felt about me perfectly clear with his hard expression in the foyer when he'd told me to come to dinner and again when he'd commented on my punctuality — something I was pretty sure had been a threat.

And yet I still thought he was gorgeous and my body

craved his arms around me. As much as I wanted to, I couldn't shake that fantasy I kept having about having sex with Cyrus. I should hate him for reminding me where I belonged and how much power he had over my life, and I did. But thoughts and feelings were two frustratingly different things and no matter what I tried, I couldn't get them to agree.

"We'll have dinner tomorrow in the summer garden," Bishop cooed, running his hand along my hair in slow, soothing strokes.

"Cyrus will expect you to dine with him." I wasn't sure if Cyrus's temper would extend to his youngest brother, but I didn't want to find out, even if I didn't want to be alone.

Except I couldn't ask any more from him. He'd spoken up for me when I knew no one would believe me.

And why would they? I was a nobody, a nothing, and they were already suspicious. There was no point in drawing more attention to myself by denying their accusations.

But they hadn't backed off, even when Bishop lied about Knox and I being fated for each other or when he'd revealed the truth about where I'd come from.

I hadn't wanted everyone to know that I was from another realm, not until after I'd started working on bringing things from my realm into this one with Whil and an engineer's help, but I'd prayed — like Bishop probably had when he'd asked me if he could tell them — that knowing the truth would shut them up or at least make their questions less aggressive and more compassionate.

Except it had only made things worse, and now I wasn't sure if it was safe to be alone in the Residence.

And I would be alone at some point.

Probably most of the time, because Bishop had work to do and Knox was on a hunt for the next three or four days and would get more hunting assignments in the future.

Given that I hadn't felt Knox's emotions since before dinner, he had to have left right after returning the picnic basket and was too far away for us to connect the way we had before.

"Cyrus will understand," Bishop said.

"He might not if it's every dinner."

"He will," Bishop insisted. "But if you're worried about it, Knox will be back in a couple of days and I suspect Nova and Deacon wouldn't mind avoiding Finn and Velora for a while." Bishop pressed his lips against the top of my head. "If you're comfortable with that."

"I ah... I don't know," I murmured.

Nova had been kind to me, even after Cyrus had yelled at me in the arena and had undoubtedly informed his betas about how I didn't know my place. She also hadn't questioned me or seemed suspicious.

In fact, she'd looked upset when Finn and Velora had started accusing me of being dangerous. Deacon had looked upset as well. Both of them knew I was from another realm, and neither of them had questioned me or suspected my intentions before or during the dinner.

Although, I hadn't really talked with Deacon. He seemed easygoing, but feralness and power radiated off him despite the laugh lines around his eyes and mouth. He could be dangerous if he wanted to be. Hell, he was the pack's huntmaster. He hunted down and fought the wild beasts in the area to help keep the pack safe. The question was, was I safe with him?

"So, want to tell me what happened?" Bishop asked after a long pause. "I thought you were getting comfortable around us."

"I am." With him and Knox. "I just— I forgot who I was when it was just the three of us. Now we're back with your pack and I needed to remember where I belonged."

"You're exactly where you belong," he said, cutting me off. "You're Knox's mate and you're going to be mine."

"I know that." I pressed my face against his chest, drawing in more of his scent to stop the tears burning my eyes. Even in the face of his betas' disapproval he still wanted me, and I couldn't thank fate enough for bringing him into my life. "I still need to remember that I'm not an alpha and never will be."

A growl rumbled in Bishop's chest. "It doesn't matter if you're an alpha. Finn, Velora, and Thane aren't alphas. Velora and Thane aren't even close, but they still have something to offer the pack. Audrey—" He nudged me back so he could look me in the eyes. "You're perfect the way you are."

My pulse stuttered and my breath caught at the affection in his eyes. It was softer than the looks he'd given me in the garden, but just as warm and soul deep, and made more tears threaten to fall.

I had no idea how I'd caught the interest of a man so kind and generous and sexy, and a part deep in my soul, a part that had momentarily grown stronger when I'd been standing in the natural stillness in the field beside the patrol shed a month ago, rose again. It brushed my consciousness for a split second, so fast I almost didn't sense it, before settling back within me.

It didn't care about the how or why Bishop was attracted to me. It just knew it was right.

"Knox, Cyrus, and I trust you and that should be more than enough for them. You won't be punished for telling them to fuck off," he assured me. "Our pack isn't like your old pack."

He kissed the tip of my nose then pulled me back to his chest. "Thane might need more than one fuck off, but he doesn't mean to badger you. He just doesn't know when his curiosity is too much for someone."

"I kind of got that impression." I closed my eyes, Bishop's steady heartbeat even more calming now that it was mixed with the feeling in my soul that being in his arms was where I belonged. "He might actually be a good person to talk to."

"He'll ask you about everything and it'll be hard to get him to stop," Bishop warned.

"But he wasn't suspicious. He was excited. He didn't

care that I came from another realm or that I was mated to Knox. He just wanted to know more about all of it." And now that I said it, I realized it was true.

I'd been nervous of Cyrus and his betas at the beginning of the meal, and that nervousness had grown to fear when they'd started accusing me of being a... spy? A danger? An I-don't-know-what-but-it-had-to-be-bad and that meant being punished.

But Thane hadn't made me feel like that at all. He reminded me of a puppy and knowledge was the bone he eagerly begged for. I just hadn't been prepared for his onslaught of questions.

"Thane has a pretty set routine and chaos ensues if you break it, so you wouldn't be able to talk to him until mid-afternoon," Bishop said, and my fear fluttered back, making my throat tighten with frustrated tears.

I wasn't supposed to be afraid. I was just supposed to be cautious until I knew I was safe with someone. And while I still wasn't sure about Nova, Deacon, or Lucius — who'd barely spoken a word — I knew without a doubt, I wasn't safe with Velora or Finn.

I also wanted to believe that I wasn't safe with Cyrus, everything told me he was dangerous, but a traitorous part of me still believed I could trust him.

Gah!

"I don't think I'm quite ready for Thane's... intensity just yet." I wanted to be brave. I desperately wanted it, but that dinner had been another reminder that I had to remain cautious. I couldn't let my guard down around someone until I knew for sure I could trust them, despite my gut instinct telling me Thane wouldn't pull rank on me.

What I needed was to prove myself. Then they'd have to respect me, or in the very least stop suspecting me.

"Bishop?" I said, suddenly too tired to care that his shirt muffled my voice. I didn't want to move from his embrace. I wanted to lie there forever, safe and warm and loved. "Is it possible to get a pen and a notebook?"

"For you, anything is possible," he replied, his words not just sounding like he'd get me what I'd asked for, but that *I* could do anything, that it was all possible.

I just needed to be brave enough.

AUDREY

I WOKE THE NEXT MORNING IN MY BED, WRAPPED IN A SOFT sheet, and completely alone. I vaguely remembered Bishop carrying me into the bedroom, lying down with me, and holding me until I fell asleep, but I didn't notice him getting up.

A small twist of disappointment tightened my stomach, but I pushed it back. Bishop had pack responsibilities and from the bright sunlight streaming through the partially closed bedroom curtains, it was well past dawn.

As much as I wanted him to, I couldn't expect him to stay in bed with me all day. He'd needed to get to work, and so did I.

I quickly showered, changed into a cream-colored shirt and tan pants, and braided my hair. The braid made me feel like I was ready to get to work and I hoped the bland clothing would make me less noticeable — since the dark green dress had done nothing to avoid Cyrus's attention. I didn't want to slink about the Residence, but I wasn't completely safe here and the more I blended into the background, the better.

With my stomach growling, since I'd barely eaten anything at dinner, I knew my first step was to find food. After that, I needed to find Bishop and get the notebook he promised, something I wasn't looking forward to.

I didn't want to aimlessly wander the Residence and possibly get in trouble, but I also didn't know who I could ask who'd know where he was.

Trying to figure out the safest way to accomplish what should have been simple goals, I strode into my sitting room to see the answers sitting on the dining room table.

I'd placed the bowl of fruit, cheese, and rolls that the older cook had insisted I take yesterday on the table, and beside it sat a leatherbound notebook and three pens.

Bishop must have brought them to my room while I was sleeping — and I wasn't going to think too hard about how I'd been alone and unconscious with my suite door unlocked.

He'd also left me a small satchel big enough for the notebook and pens and a few other things like a wallet, which reminded me of how much I didn't have and just how dependent I was on him.

I didn't feel safe wandering around town. Lucius had said last night that the pack was already talking about me and Knox, and I didn't want to risk the rest of the pack reacting like the betas had. But even if I did feel safe, there wasn't much I could do. I had no money so I couldn't buy myself food or even just a trinket that made me happy.

And while Bishop hadn't used money with the shopkeepers when he'd bought me clothes, other people had exchanged coins for their purchases. The alphas probably had free rein over what they wanted or they had expense accounts and the bills were sent to the Residence. It wasn't like everyone didn't know where they lived or something.

I didn't want to stay dependent on Bishop, Knox, or anyone else, which meant I needed to come up with good information soon and get Bishop to convince Cyrus to pay me for it.

That thought left a sour taste in my mouth. Would Cyrus even consider paying me? Or would he say I cost them money walking to the death god's temple and was paying off my debt?

It was going to be like living with Merrick all over again. Cyrus was going to say I needed to work for him to pay him back for living at the Residence, and I'd never earn my own money.

I bit back a growl of frustration. I'd sworn I'd never go back to that and I wouldn't. If Cyrus was going to demand my labor for room and board without any extra compensation, I'd find a cheaper place to live. It might even be safer than staying at the Residence.

Knox would be pissed, of course, but I could probably convince him it was for the best, especially if I found a place near the edge of town where we could spend time together.

I might even be able to convince Bishop it was what I needed, too. I'd never been on my own before, never been free.

My heart sank. All of that was only if Cyrus allowed it and he'd never allow it.

What was the point of even trying? He'd never let me go all in the name of protecting his brothers. If I begged, would Knox and Bishop even be able to get Cyrus to listen to them?

And the God damned frustrating part of me that was somehow attracted to Cyrus and fantasized about him didn't want to leave at all.

Damn it! A week ago, I wouldn't have had this fear. Cyrus had asked about my plans for the future, had seemed to care about me. Then in a flash, he'd acted like Merrick and all that confidence in him and the others vanished.

I trusted too easily because I didn't want to believe all alphas were like Merrick, Sterling, and Royce. On TV, alphas were heroic and protective. And yes, it was foolish to think there was any truth in a TV show, movie, or book.

But just like I'd foolishly hoped there was someone out there who'd love me for me, despite all my weaknesses, I'd hoped I'd find a pack where I wasn't the alpha's slave.

And I *had* found it. The first part at least. Bishop wanted me for me. But that only kept a glimmer of hope alive for Cyrus and the idea that if I proved myself, he'd accept me. He'd respect me.

He'd care about me.

Praying that proving myself would set me free, I bit into one of the apples, opened the notebook to make notes, and tapped my pen on the paper. All the things I thought the pack might find useful rushed through my head and I realized I had no idea what the pack knew and didn't know.

I knew they didn't know about photography and movies, but did they know about electricity — even on a basic level — or what about light and sound waves?

It didn't look like they had a whole lot of sophisticated medical equipment — which as shifters they didn't really need — but did they know about blood pressure or the spinal cord or nearsightedness?

If they didn't know about vision problems, did they know about concave and convex lenses that could magnify things or help them see things far away?

The list went on and on, and I was going to have to talk to someone and figure out what they did and didn't know. Bishop wouldn't have the time, not with how much I needed to know and how fast I wanted it. But would anyone else help me?

My thoughts jumped to Whil. Maybe she'd be willing to help. She'd been nothing but kind to me. Although after Cyrus had turned suddenly into Merrick, I had more evidence that I couldn't trust my own judgment of people.

I'd approach her cautiously. If she reacted badly then I'd know she'd talked with Cyrus and agreed with him.

If not, spending time with her, even if it was just drinking tea while she worked, would ease my too-on-edge nerves and help me think. I'd gotten the impression not a lot of people visited her cottage library greenhouse at the back of the Residence's ground. That would limit the nasty looks I'd get from people or the fear that someone was going to teach me a lesson.

Someone knocked on my door, startling me and making my pulse lurch then race at a furious pace.

"Audrey?" Nova called through the door. "Are you up?"

I released the breath I hadn't realized I was holding. Nova, for now, was safe. She could still turn on me, but nothing in her behavior suggested she would and she was even polite enough to knock and ask first before opening the door.

"I'm up," I called as I hurried to answer the door.

"Are you hungry?" she asked, her critical gaze sliding over me.

Worry fluttered through my chest for a second, but quickly vanished. I didn't feel like she was judging me, not like Velora and Finn had at dinner last night. It was more like she was assessing my health.

"The other betas have left the kitchen so I thought now would be a perfect time." Her attention jumped past my shoulder to the table. "But I see you've already found food."

"The older woman in the kitchen gave me the bowl last night." But confessing that only reminded me of Cyrus's comments about it. "She wouldn't take no for an answer," I mumbled.

Nova chuckled, clearly hearing everything I said with her better-than-human hearing.

"Yeah, Eloise is like that," she said, affection warming her voice. "If you'd like a warm breakfast, I have no doubt she'll want to cook something for you."

That had been my impression of the older cook as well as the younger one. They'd also seemed concerned for me at dinner last night.

I glanced at the barely eaten apple in my hand and the bowl of food on the table. If I had something more substantial now, I could save what was in the bowl for when I really needed it.

"Come on," Nova said. "I have half an hour before my next meeting. I'll keep you company."

"Thank you." I instinctually dropped my gaze and Nova huffed, making me cringe.

"Head up, Audrey," Nova scolded. "You're Knox's mate and you have more right to be here than they do."

I shoved my notebook and pens into the satchel,

grabbed the apple I'd taken a bite out of, and forced my gaze to meet Nova's.

In return, she offered me a brilliant smile and held the door open.

"There's something you need to know about Cyrus," she said as we headed down the hall to the kitchen. "About all of the brothers, actually. They're extremely powerful alphas."

I nodded even though any idiot would have been able to see they were powerful.

"I have a hypersensitivity to alpha power, so I can feel how powerful they are even when they're controlling it." Her gaze slid to mine. "I suspect you can feel it, too."

For a split-second I contemplated denying it, but it didn't matter if Nova knew I could sense someone's power level or not and it would be a small way to test her sincerity. I didn't know how she or anyone could use the information against me, but Sterling would have figured out a way, which meant someone else could as well.

"I can," I replied softly.

"Alphas with that amount of power have a stronger connection with their wolf and it makes it harder to control their instincts."

Ah, so this was the excuse for her alpha's behavior conversation.

"And no, this isn't an excuse," she continued as if she could read my mind. "It's an explanation. Bishop deals with his wolf freaking out by being the life of the party, Knox doesn't deal with it at all, just lets it take over, and

Cyrus fights so hard to regain control he sometimes hurts the people around him. I know Cyrus yelled at you and I can assume he said some pretty awful things."

"I'd forgotten my place and he reminded me. It won't happen again."

Nova sighed. "Knowing Cyrus, it probably will, but it has nothing to do with your place in this pack. It's all about Cyrus and his wolf freaking out because he failed to protect you."

We turned down the hall toward the kitchen, its door twenty feet away, and Nova grabbed my arm.

"You did nothing wrong," she insisted.

"I didn't think."

"Your mate was in danger and you did what your instincts told you. You didn't step out of line because there isn't a line like that in this pack. You're not a servant or slave or lesser than anyone else."

I opened my mouth to protest that part, but she cut me off.

"You're not lesser and if you can sense power like I think you can, you have an ability that very few in this pack have." Her expression turned wry. "Cyrus will apologize. It'll be long after you've gotten over it and moved on, but he'll get his head out of his ass eventually."

I nodded, not sure what to say to that or if I even believed it.

Regardless, I still didn't have proof that it was safe enough to let my guard down around him or almost anyone else.

Nova's wry expression softened with affection and a hint of sadness. She could tell I didn't completely believe her. But she didn't press the matter, likely knowing I needed concrete evidence and that would take time to get.

AUDREY

Nova stayed and chatted with me while Eloise made me an omelet and the younger cook, Kira, poured me a glass of sweet, pink juice and cut my apple into pieces. We talked about the pack, the things I could see and do in town — once my doctor-appointed rest was complete — and where I should get Bishop and Knox to take me.

I learned the pack was almost completely self-sufficient and its primary exports were hunters and the healing elixirs, both of which were in short supply. They didn't mass produce anything, and I didn't know if that was because they didn't want to, didn't know they could, or couldn't.

Time ran out before I could ask Nova about medical equipment and she hurried off to her meeting, leaving me with Eloise and Kira who were happy to talk about their kitchen and how they prepared food.

They were so warm and friendly and excited about

their work that I didn't realize it was lunchtime until Deacon walked in, startling me.

"You're still here," he exclaimed to Eloise and Kira as I tried to subtly shy away from him. "Shouldn't you be on break or shopping?"

"We were telling Audrey about our kitchen," Kira replied with a brilliant smile as if no one had asked her about her work before.

Deacon's gaze slid to mine, and I plastered on my most submissive expression and found a spot on the wall beside his head that I could look at. I didn't want to risk my gut instinct being wrong about him. Better to err on the side of caution.

"I didn't realize it was lunchtime," I said. "Excuse me. I don't want to disturb you." And I really didn't want to still be there when Finn and Velora showed up.

"You're so quiet, I doubt you'd disturb a mouse," Deacon replied.

I glanced at Eloise and Kira, who were frowning.

"Thank you," I told them.

"You better come back tomorrow," Eloise said. "I was just about to give you a tour of the herb garden and show you my favorite recipe." Her worry bloomed into a warm, inviting smile, the kind of smile a mother might give her child, something I'd seen but never experienced before.

"I will," I assured her and rushed out the back door into brilliant hot sunshine, buzzing insects, chirping birds, and fragrant air. For a moment, I'd felt free and safe and comfortable. Eloise's and Kira's excitement over cooking was contagious and I wanted more of that feeling.

Hoping I'd receive the same welcome with Whil, I followed the path through the herb garden, past the Residence's private sacred grove to Whil's greenhouse-English cottage-library.

Trees and bushes and all manner of flowers crowded around the strange building. It didn't seem to matter that it was summer, tulips and irises bloomed beside daisies and daylilies and fall chrysanthemums and dahlias.

Much to my surprise, Whil, the most beautiful woman I'd ever seen with her long golden hair, delicately pointed ears, and perpetual soft golden fae glow, was outside picking berries from a bush near the back.

I walked toward her, my pace getting slower and slower, my nerves making my heart race.

She wasn't pack so she might not feel the same way about me as other shifters.

Please, let that be true.

"Audrey!" Whil's face brightened the moment she saw me, flooding me with relief. "You've got to try these. They're the closest I can get to a berry I loved in Fairy and this is the only bush in the area."

The bush wasn't very big, standing as high as my waist and only a few feet wider than me. It was heavy with small, bright pink berries but they were still only enough to make three, maybe four pies, and likely wouldn't even fill her medium-sized bucket.

"If you love them so much, why wouldn't you grow

more?" I asked as Whil lifted the basket, offering me her precious fruit.

"A merchant brought the plant to Stonehaven from a much warmer land about two hundred years ago, and trust me, I've tried to make it grow bigger, tried to grow cuttings, tried everything I could think of."

I popped the berry in my mouth, letting the juice coat my tongue before swallowing it. It tasted like strawberries and cream, and I couldn't hold back a soft moan. "It's so good."

"I told you," she said with a grin. "I think the only reason it's alive is because it's here and I unconsciously make things grow in a fifty-foot radius around my cottage despite the weather."

"Does it make berries all the time?"

Whil sighed. "Only twice a year so I make sure I pick them before any of them go bad. Come! I have the perfect tea for these."

She led me back to the entrance to her greenhouse library and its inside garden, just as vibrant as the flowering garden outside. The strange combination still astounded me with the bookshelves crammed with books and scrolls and jars, making secret nooks and standing among a cacophony of colorful flowers, even though the ceiling and walls were glass like an ordinary greenhouse.

As she led me farther across the uneven flagstone floor and past the strange steps that went nowhere in the middle of a small gurgling pool, the glass turned into a mix of glass windows and stone walls and the ceiling became a normal ceiling. More bookshelves lined the walls, creating more secret little nooks partially hidden by foliage and begging to be explored.

Whil took me to the back to the mismatched seating area consisting of two simple wooden chairs, a stool, a chair with thick cushions, and an old-fashioned couch with only one arm. Piles of books littered the area, and I couldn't tell if she'd moved anything from when I'd first visited her greenhouse a month ago.

She set the basket of berries on the table between the various seats and hurried around a corner into the cottage part of her house, the dimmer light making her golden glow more obvious.

I sat on the old-fashioned couch stunned. I'd planned to approach her cautiously and find out how she felt about me. Instead, she'd welcomed me like a long-lost friend and now I was sitting in her home awaiting tea so I could eat her precious berries.

Had Cyrus not talked to her?

It was possible, which meant the next time I visited, I might not be so welcome. But then again, maybe not. Maybe Whil liked me like Eloise and Kira did.

"Here we are," Whil announced as she reentered carrying a silver tray with two tall glasses and a pitcher filled with a pale green liquid.

She set the tray beside the basket, filled both glasses, and sat on the floor opposite me surrounded by uneven stacks of books.

"You've had quite a journey," she said. "I'm sorry the

spell didn't work and you had to seal your bond with Knox. And I'm sorry Cyrus was an idiot and lost his temper."

So she did know what had happened. But did she know what he'd actually said or how he really felt about me?

She must have seen something in my expression because hers softened and she pushed the basket of berries closer to me.

"Cyrus comes from a long line of protectors and sometimes they can mistake overbearing for protecting." She took a long sip of her cold tea and studied me. "It doesn't excuse what he did. He owes you an enormous apology. I just hope knowing this helps you see that it wasn't your fault."

I nodded and took my own sip of tea to avoid saying anything, surprised at the sweet minty taste of the beverage. Nova had said something similar and while I could see overprotectiveness being Cyrus's reason for yelling at me, it was safer to assume I'd displeased him and try not to do it again in the future.

"I'm sure you have questions about the tether and the blocking magic I used to prevent whoever is on the other end from influencing you," she said changing the conversation.

A shudder swept through me. I'd been so worried about Cyrus, I'd forgotten that Sterling could make me dream horrible things and manipulate me.

"Bishop said the block wasn't permanent." That was

the biggest thing I was worried about. How sturdy was the block? Would it fade away or just vanished leaving me susceptible to Sterling's manipulations?

"Correct, it isn't permanent," Whil replied, her expression turning grim. "I'm not sure how long the block will last so I'd like to check it regularly so we can get an idea of the tether's strength. Thankfully the tether isn't a true bond so there are other ways to break it besides going back to the death god's temple."

"There are?" I leaned toward her, a small flicker of hope bursting to life inside me.

I could finally be free of Sterling.

"I found some possible options while I was looking for a way to break your mating bond."

Except Bishop hadn't mentioned anything about breaking the tether yesterday, which meant Whil hadn't told him or he'd decided not to tell me. Either option indicated that these ways to break the tether were long shots, just like breaking the mating bond.

"Would you let me take a closer look at the tether? I was in a hurry when I blocked it and I doubted Knox would have let me stick around after you were safe. I'm actually surprised about the number of people he let help you." Whil chuckled softly. "The power of a sealed mating bond, I guess."

"I guess so," I replied, the sudden mention of Knox making my chest ache. He hadn't even been gone a full day and I already missed the feel of his emotions whispering through our bond.

"So..." Whil popped two more berries into her mouth. "Can I look at that tether?"

"Please." If it finally got Sterling out of my life for good, I'd do just about anything.

Whil sat on the old-fashioned couch beside me and placed her palms against my temples. Warmth radiated from her skin and into my head, and a gold light filled my vision.

"Take a breath," she ordered, making me realize I'd been holding it. "This won't hurt. It'll probably make you drowsy. Just relax."

I drew in a deep breath and slowly let it out, sinking into the warmth and golden glow of her magic. A soft haze muddled my thoughts and I knew I was completely helpless against Whil or anyone else who entered the greenhouse library.

But I also knew in my soul that I was safe with her. It was as if her magic connected me to her, and just like I knew I was safe with Knox and he was my mate, I could tell Whil didn't have ill intentions toward me. In fact, she saw me as a kind of kindred spirit. We were both outsiders to the pack in our own way, separated from our homes, and didn't fit easily into the pack's hierarchy. The realization let me fall deeper into her golden warmth.

A moment later, the warmth withdrew and I opened my eyes. Except I wasn't sitting on the old-fashioned couch anymore, I was lying on it and Whil sat on the floor near one of her bookcases with a large tome open on her lap.

"Good," she said. "You're awake just in time for dinner."

My pulse lurched and I jerked upright.

Dinner? I slept all afternoon?

And hell, dinner! I didn't want to have dinner in the dining room again. Bishop had promised I wouldn't have to, but I didn't know where he was, and if he hadn't talked to Cyrus, I'd get in trouble for not showing up.

I tried to suck in a calming breath. I really really didn't want to go, but it would be safest to dress, present myself, and suffer through another meal. Now that I knew I had Bishop, Whil, and possibly Nova on my side, I had a better chance of keeping my expression pleasant when interrogated by the others.

"Bishop said to meet him in the summer garden," Whil said, sending a blast of relief flooding through me before it jerked to panic.

Bishop wanted to see me again in the summer garden. We'd had sex there the last time and I really hoped it meant we'd have sex again, but I wasn't ready. I was in a shirt and pants again, not a pretty dress and—

I ran a hand over my hair.

Yep, half of it had fallen out of my braid while I'd slept.

I had to look like a complete mess.

"When do I need to meet him?" Maybe I could run back to my room to freshen up.

"He said whenever it got close to dinner time or you woke up."

"So now?" I squeaked. I didn't know why I was suddenly so nervous. It wasn't like we hadn't had sex before *and* while I'd been wearing the exact same outfit. "I could have slept through the night."

I quickly rebraided my hair. I had to get ahold of myself. I was making too much of his invitation. He might not want sex. He might just want to eat a meal with me.

"Calm down," Whil chuckled. "I'm pretty sure he's already madly in love with you."

"What? He's not— I— You can tell?" Could everyone? I knew he hadn't made an attempt to hide his intentions, but—

But nothing. He wasn't hiding and neither should I.

I thanked Whil for the tea and berries and, with my heart racing in anticipation, I rushed to the herb garden near the kitchen so I could find my way to the summer garden.

AUDREY

Bishop wasn't there when I arrived, but he'd told Whil he'd meet me there and he'd never broken his word to me, so I sat underneath the pergola and all its gorgeous flowering vines. A gentle breeze *shushed* through the foliage, easing the summer heat and making the bands of early evening sunshine dance on the soft grass around me.

The bright yellow glow of a summer afternoon had deepened into a rich gold, edged with oranges and reds, and for a moment, it felt like summer back on Earth. The cicadas were buzzing, the air was warm and thick, and the soft breeze brought quick breaths of contrasting coolness.

Except I'd never felt as at home there as I did here. Even with my worry about Cyrus and the rest of the pack, I felt like this realm was where I belonged.

Footsteps crunched on the gravel path and I tensed,

my gaze jumping up to watch Bishop stride through the wrought iron arch. Just the sight of him stole my breath, and his radiant smile when he saw me sucked all the air from the garden.

He was happy to see me. Me. Awkward, weak me.

I didn't think I'd ever get used to that.

The smile turned heated the closer he got and I could hear the handle of the wicker basket in his grip creak as he tightened his hold.

"I promised myself we'd eat first this time," he said, his voice gruff, sending a shiver of desire racing down my spine.

"Do you have anywhere else to be after dinner?" I asked, my tone just as husky and filled with invitation.

"No."

"Then it doesn't matter when we eat." I mentally gaped at my words. I didn't know where I'd found the confidence to flirt with him like that again, but I liked it.

Bishop dropped to his knees. He captured my lips in a demanding kiss and the shiver of desire he'd inspired when he'd stepped into the garden exploded into desperate need.

Oh, yes. This was what I hadn't realized I'd been craving all day right from the moment I'd woken in an empty bed.

I tangled my fingers in his jaw-length hair and kissed him back just as wildly. Our tongues fought for dominance, our teeth clacked together in our passion, and his hands were everywhere. They tugged at my hair, stroked over my breasts, and slid to my ass. Arms, thighs, back, neck, stomach as if he couldn't get enough of me. It ignited every nerve in my body until I was aching and panting and desperate for him.

"I've been thinking about you all day," he gasped, pulling up for air and pressing his forehead against mine. "Haven't been able to concentrate on anything."

His hands swept under my shirt, teasing up my already sensitive flesh until he reached my breasts, where he palmed them roughly. Hungry for more contact, I arched into his touch. I needed more, needed him, needed everything.

It had surprised me the first time Bishop had kissed me with almost the same wildness as my dream-Knox. I'd always thought he'd be a gentle lover all the time, and I loved how careful he was with me. But I also loved when he let go. It made me feel like he couldn't be without me, that he needed me with the same overwhelming desire my dream-Knox had needed me.

I nipped at his jaw, drawing a low rumble in his chest that sent wet heat rushing to my core.

"Fuck, you smell so good." He yanked off my shirt, his eyes fully dark as if his wolf was taking over, and raked his gaze over my naked breasts.

The urge to cover my nudity and my scars dampened my desire, but it only lasted a second. Bishop didn't look at me with disgust or pity. He never had. He looked like he wanted to devour me and couldn't figure out where to start first, and my reaction was just an old habit that I really hoped I'd break soon.

With a groan, he dipped down and swept his tongue over my right breast with a heavy, slow stroke. My nipple instantly hardened and my breath caught as desire zinged through me.

"Mine," he growled, his voice so much like Knox's that I realized it wasn't Bishop pleasuring me, but his wolf... which was more than fine with me. We'd never be able to have a lasting relationship if his wolf didn't want me and I really wanted a relationship with Bishop.

He scraped his partially extended canines over my sensitive flesh then sucked the aching bud into his mouth. The pull verged on painful and yet the throbbing in my core intensified and I could feel my desire leaking down my thighs.

Moaning, I clung to him as he nipped and sucked one nipple then the other, the rumble in his chest getting louder and louder, vibrating with delicious pleasure straight to my core.

The ache within me swelled and I was on the verge of a climax with just him sucking my nipples. But he pulled away before I fell over the edge.

I groaned with disappointment but he quickly undid my pants, yanked them to my knees, and buried his face between my legs.

Oh, yes!

My orgasm swelled right to the edge, and I trembled

as if I was about to crash into bliss. But I needed one more lick or suck or something.

"Bishop, please." I bucked my hips, trying to get the friction I needed on my clit to throw me over the edge.

But he clamped his hands on my hips instead, holding me still and making me writhe and whine in frustration.

Just a little more. Please.

The ache inside me just kept building. Why wasn't he doing anything? Why was he just breathing in my scent like he needed it to survive?

"Mine," he growled as he glanced up at me.

His canines were fully extended and hints of his wolf sharpened his features. The wildness in his eyes set off a mini orgasm, just a tease of what I knew was coming, not enough for relief, and his lips curled into a smirk. He knew exactly what he was doing to me.

In that moment, he looked like Knox, but I knew I hadn't mistaken the twins for each other. I knew he wasn't my bonded mate. I couldn't feel this man's emotions. I could only see them in the intensity in his eyes. And his eyes said that this was one hundred percent Bishop's wolf, the primal nature of his soul, and that his wolf was hungry for me.

"Yours," I told him and in my heart, I knew it was true.

I belonged with Knox *and* Bishop. Somehow, I just *knew* they were both my mates. And while yes, I wanted to wait on mating with Bishop so he could court me and make me feel loved and special, I'd also already fallen in love with him. I'd fallen the moment he'd held me in Kelna and swore he wanted to mate with me even if I was weak and couldn't shift and was already mated to Knox.

The look in Bishop's eyes turned into a victorious gleam and he roughly licked my clit, sending stars shooting across my vision.

The orgasm was violent and quick, but he didn't let up, licking and sucking me straight into another orgasm and another. My mind spun with pleasure, my breath was ragged, and I didn't care what noises I made or who could hear them.

Bishop's wolf was relentless, turning me into a moaning, gasping mess. He flipped me to my stomach and yanked my pants off before I'd even fully realized we'd changed position. Then he jerked my hips up and plunged his cock into me in one ferocious thrust.

The impact of our bodies colliding rattled down my spine and pushed me hard into the ground, but I didn't care. The rush of him inside me, the force of his need, just made this moment even better.

He withdrew and slammed into me again and again, faster, harder, wilder, claiming my body with his delicious, merciless attack.

I strained to catch my breath, stars flashing behind my lids with the promise of an earth-shattering release. The heated need that I'd thought was satiated from all the oral sex, roared into a raging inferno of desperate desire.

I clawed at the ground, digging my nails into the grass

and dirt, and screamed with every ferocious thrust. It
created a wildness within me that I'd only felt during my
dreams about Knox, and I shoved my ass back, meeting
Bishop's thrust, submitting to its need. And it needed to
claim Bishop as my own, needed him deep within my
body, fucking me until I couldn't see straight.

"More," I gasped at Bishop's wolf. "Harder."

The wildness surged and so did my pleasure. This
was what I wanted. What I hadn't *known* I'd wanted. To
be completely claimed by Bishop, to have his body mark
mine, if not with a bite, then with a wonderful ache that
would last for days. "More more more."

I hadn't thought I was ready for rough sex like I'd had
in my dreams, not with how big Bishop's cock was, but
half a dozen quick orgasms were enough to make me
slick and ready, and I never wanted it to end. I wanted to
fly on this high forever. I wanted to seize my power, a
power that had this incredible, strong shifter, unable to
control himself.

With a growl, Bishop clasped a hand around my
throat and arched my back, his cock hitting a new spot
within me that made electric need zap through me,
stealing all breath and sight and sound.

"Yes," I screamed.

"Mine," he snarled and he pinched my clit with a
sharp, painful twist with his free hand.

I completely shattered, screaming my release like a
wild animal, the sensation too strong to keep in. Every
muscle in my body clenched tight, pleasure flooding into

my very essence and I whirled on violent flashes of light and ecstasy.

Bishop stiffened and howled with his own release, the sound more like a wolf than a man, and his canines grazed my neck. It was on the opposite shoulder of Knox's mating marks, the only scars I should have had as a shifter.

Yes, I mentally begged. *Make me yours forever.*

In that moment, I didn't care that he'd barely courted me. I wanted him more than I'd wanted anything in my life.

Somehow, he managed to control his wolf and not bite me, sending a sliver of disappointment oozing through my bliss.

"Soon," he murmured, his voice human again as he clutched me tight.

A violent aftershock swept through me, burning away my disappointment, and I collapsed against his chest

"Soon," I agreed and his wolf rumbled his pleasure.

Soon this powerful alpha would be mine. Just like he was supposed to be. Just like fate demanded.

AUDREY

THE NEXT FOUR DAYS WERE PLEASANTLY SIMILAR TO THE previous one. Nova or Bishop took me to breakfast after the other betas had eaten, then they headed to work. I stayed and chatted with Eloise and Kira, learning more about the pack, its recent history, and what living in Stonehaven was like.

The pack was more alive and vibrant than my old pack, and that wasn't just because I'd been ostracized or because it was a quarter of the size. The Stonehaven pack had more than two restaurants and a single bar. It had six restaurants and seven pubs, a couple of dance halls, a theatre for plays, and a community center that always had something happening morning, afternoon, and evening. There was also the arena that hosted events that the whole pack would be interested in like traveling musicians or acting troupes or sporting events among the pack.

It was clear by how she talked about the pack that Eloise loved it and the people. Kira loved it as well, but I could sense every time she mentioned something outside the pack that she wanted to see new sights and sounds and, more importantly, learn new dishes.

As we talked, I helped wash the breakfast dishes or prepare the informal lunch that those working and living in the Residence could eat whenever their schedules allowed it.

Then, before the betas arrived to grab their lunches, I headed to the back of the grounds to Whil's cottage where she studied the tether — usually knocking me out for the rest of the day — or answered my questions about what scientific and engineering discoveries the pack had made and about their magical items.

I had no doubt that they used magic for more than just their lights and discovered their fridges and freezers had magical cold stones and every faucet had hot and cold stone chips to heat or cool the water temperature.

My evenings ended with dinner in my suite. Much to my disappointment, Bishop couldn't eat with me the first two nights, but Nova and then Nova and Deacon kept me company, and neither of them looked at me with suspicion or made me feel threatened.

Last night, I'd had Bishop all to myself again and we mostly ate our spicy chicken and pasta dinner before falling into my bed and making love.

Now I stood at the open gate to the Residence's grounds waiting for Bishop to take me to the community center — which also happened to be Stonehaven's school — where Nova was teaching her first aid class.

It was just past lunch and I shifted from foot to foot, unable to hold in my nervousness. On one hand, I was excited to finally be able to explore the town and was eagerly awaiting Knox's return sometime today.

On the other hand, I'd started feeling safe in my quiet, reclusive routine. I'd managed to successfully avoid running into Velora, Finn, and Thane, and, most importantly, Cyrus.

A shiver of desire skated down my spine just like it always did when I thought of Cyrus and the fantasy of having sex with him flooded my mind.

God, when was it going to go away?

I couldn't believe I was still thinking about it even after having three glorious sexual encounters — not to mention numerous orgasms — with Bishop.

I wanted to scream in frustration. I was happy with Bishop, and while I barely knew Knox, I knew I'd be happy with him, too. I certainly didn't need to be fantasizing about their older brother.

Footsteps thudded on the flagstone driveway and I looked up, my pulse suddenly twice as fast as it had been a moment ago and my body heating.

"Bish—" I started then realized it was Cyrus who was marching toward me.

My pulse picked up even faster, no longer spurred by desire, and a cold dread sank heavy into my stomach.

This was the first time I'd spoken with him since that disastrous dinner — and I was definitely speaking to him because there was nowhere to hide and from the hard set of his jaw, he'd already spotted me.

"Leaving the Residence?" he asked, his voice gruff as he approached. "Do you have Nova's permission?"

I dropped my gaze and strained to school my expression into a pleasant mask. "I do, alpha. She asked me to attend her first aid class."

"And you're waiting for Bishop to escort you?"

"Yes, alpha."

A hint of his power stuttered over me. The need to look at him seized me, but it vanished just as quickly, saving me from getting an eyeful of him and reigniting my fantasy.

But as soon as I realized that—

I shoved the fantasy as far back in my mind as I could and concentrated on all the cracks and grooves in the stone driveway beneath my feet.

I don't think he's sexy. I don't think he's sexy. God, why couldn't I make myself believe that?

He'd put me in my place and clearly didn't want to even be around a weakling like me.

"I just saw Velora ambush him with the final last details for tomorrow's festival," Cyrus said, making something sour curl around my heart. "I doubt he'll be free until dinner."

Disappointment joined the sour sensation, surprising

me. I hadn't realized just how much I wanted to see Bishop or how much I didn't want him hanging around Velora. Which was ridiculous. Bishop wasn't interested in Velora. He was interested in me.

"Thank you for telling me, alpha," I said, managing to keep my voice steady. "Excuse me."

I turned to head to Whil's cottage. If Bishop wasn't coming, there was no point in continuing to wait. I'd find out when Nova was teaching her next first aid class and try to join again.

"Where are you going?" Cyrus demanded, his words freezing me in place despite him not using any of his power.

Shit. I hadn't asked to be excused and left before he'd given me permission.

I turned back to him, my gaze back on my feet and my hands clasped in front of me.

Shit shit shit.

I'd dropped my guard, just for a moment because Bishop, Nova, and Deacon, as well as Whil, Eloise, and Kira had made me feel safe. Now I'd given Cyrus a reason to discipline me.

"Don't you want to take the first aid class?" he asked.

"I..." I couldn't tell from his tone if he wanted me to say yes or no. When we'd been traveling, he'd suggested it, but that was before he'd reminded me of my position in the pack.

He huffed. "Come on. I'm meeting with some merchants here for the festival. The school is on my way."

He turned on his heel and headed through the gate, his posture rigid and a muscle in his jaw twitching.

Confused, I hurried after him. Was he trying to make me useful for the pack, or was he actually being nice?

Either way, he told me to follow, and I couldn't disobey him.

Cyrus took the most direct path into town, his pace almost too quick for me as if he couldn't stand being with me and wanted to get our walk over and done with. He followed the main road through Old Town and halfway into the newer part of Stonehaven before taking a right onto another prominent road to a large, three-story building.

The building had decorative scrollwork at its eaves and around the windows and door as well as large bricks, suggesting it wasn't one of the newer buildings, but it also had the newer buildings' style of large windows, making it a beautiful blending of old and new.

It sat butted against a granite slope that had been carved to make long, wide steps. The steps curved around an area paved with flagstones that had a few stone benches and tables, along with three patches of white marks — each patch a different pattern — and a large white circle in the center, reminding me of a school playground. Beside the paved area lay a grassed area with a jungle gym that looked to be a mix of human obstacles and ones suited to wolf pups.

Both areas were shaded by towering oaks and both

had a few large stone planters marking the edges and filled with colorful flowers.

Cyrus strode across the paved area and straight through the front door, and I scrambled to catch up with him, surprised he hadn't just left me and worried about what going inside with me meant.

AUDREY

THE INSIDE OF THE SCHOOL/COMMUNITY CENTER LOOKED like a regular school without any people in it. There were open doors at regular intervals, revealing empty classrooms, and smaller halls breaking off from the main one to get to more classrooms.

In the center of the building was a grand foyer with a wide staircase, similar to the one in the Residence. The stairs swept up all three stories in the same meet halfway break apart to a landing on either side of the building style. It'd be a pain in the ass if you had classes on both sides of the building and had to go down half a flight and back up to reach the other, but it looked spectacular.

I could hear the soft sounds of people talking from somewhere in the building, but I didn't see anyone and could only assume it was the weekend or summer break or something since it was just after lunch and there should have been classes going.

The voices, however, grew louder the closer we got to the back of the school. Here, the rooms had more of an office look with long rectangular or wide circular tables, and more comfortable looking chairs. Or they were completely empty of furniture with large rugs on the floor instead of the polished stone in the rest of the building.

"Here," Cyrus said as he stopped at an open door and gestured for me to enter.

"Thank you, alpha," I murmured as I stepped into the room.

All conversation in the room stopped and everyone stared at me.

Then Cyrus stepped in behind me and all the eyes rose a foot and a half above my head.

"Where's Nova?" he asked.

"Got hung up at the hospital. Said she'd be here in about ten minutes," a very familiar looking young man said.

Why did he look familiar?

Oh! The guy from the road on the outskirts of town when Bishop and I had returned from our long journey north. He'd told me his name... but as much as I wracked my brain, I couldn't remember it.

"Good." Cyrus turned on his heel and strode back down the hall, leaving me in a room full of strangers. Strangers who were looking at me with an unsettling mix of emotions.

Swell.

Everyone was seated around a circular table, and, if the chairs between people were any indication, they were separated into three groups.

The group closest to me consisted of three girls and two guys. They looked to be around my age, maybe a year or two younger, and had the darkest, most unnerving expressions. But I didn't know if they didn't like me because they were friends or family of Velora or Finn, or just because I was a stranger.

The group to my left, who were older, mid-thirties, had two women and two men. From the way they were sitting together, it looked like they were two mated pairs. They looked intensely curious, reminding me too much of Thane and his barrage of questions.

The final group, to my right and closer to the back, consisted of the guy I'd met the other night whose name I couldn't remember and a tiny woman with a soft, kind, smile.

"I've got a seat right here for you, Audrey," the guy said, pushing out the chair beside him and making my cheeks heat with embarrassment because he'd remembered my name and I couldn't remember his.

"Thank you." I hurried around the table and sat, my pulse picking up as people continued to stare at me.

From the alpha power radiating off them, one of the women in the group of four and the nice guy beside me were the strongest, although neither of them were close to my guys' or Cyrus's strength. The others were still stronger than me, but not by so much that I wouldn't be able to resist their compulsion.

"Jeez, guys," Nice Guy said. "Why don't you introduce yourselves instead of staring."

One of the women in the group of five who had black hair and piercing green eyes huffed. "I want to know why the alpha personally escorted her here."

"Yeah," the guy beside her said. He had matching black hair and green eyes and was probably her brother. "He's got more important things to do, especially after taking off with her for a month."

The other woman in the group who reminded me of a slightly younger version of Velora with her dark hair and similar bone structure nodded her agreement, her stare edged with a hint of jealousy.

"I—" I started then stopped myself before I told them Bishop was supposed to have escorted me.

Given how all the other women seemed interested in Bishop and how Velora's possible sister or cousin or whatever she was had looked after I'd shown up with Cyrus, it probably wasn't smart to mention I also spent time with Bishop. Sure it was going to come out sooner or later — like tomorrow when we walked around the festival together — that Bishop was courting me to be his mate, but I'd rather make the confession with at least one person I trusted in the room with me.

"Is it true you're mated to Knox?" a bulky guy in the foursome asked.

"Of course it's true," the black-haired green-eyed guy said. "He wouldn't have lost his shit like that and run deeper into town if she hadn't been his mate."

"My uncle saw it all," one of the girls in the foursome said. She was gorgeous and curvy and I was shocked that no one in the room was giving her a second look. Perhaps it was because she seemed almost as shy as me. "He's never seen Knox act like that before and it was definitely the behavior of a bonded mate."

"So what's she doing with Cyrus?" asked Female Green Eyes from the group of five — now dubbed the Nasty group in my mind because they were the first group I'd noticed and no one was sharing their name.

"Knox is on a hunt," I said, looking up but not making eye contact with any of them. I didn't know if it was smart to offer an explanation but no one here was an alpha and the strongest wolf in the room was Nice Guy. "Cyrus has a meeting in town and said the community center was on his way."

Not-Velora frowned and crossed her arms. "But he came in and checked the room."

"I saw that too," a guy from Nasty added. He had shaggy blond hair and a slim figure, and the third girl in the group, just as skinny as him, leaned against his shoulder and possessively clung to his arm.

Nice Guy rolled his eyes. "Of course he did. One of the foreigners attacked her. He'd do the same for any of us."

Shy girl of the more neutral foursome glanced up at me with a sad smile. "My uncle said she hurt herself."

"That's what I heard," Not-Velora agreed.

"She's mated to Knox. Would you blame her?" the black-haired guy asked. Everyone stiffened and my stomach churned with the clashing urges to stand up for Knox and not draw even more attention to myself.

Nice Guy growled low in his throat, his bright green eyes darkening as his wolf rose to the surface. "He's your alpha and you just insulted him in front of his mate." The rumble in his chest deepened and he leaned forward. "If you want to get hurt so badly become a hunter or join the watch."

Black-haired Guy's eyes widened as if suddenly realizing what he'd said. "I'm sorry, alpha."

Alpha? Was he talking to Nice Guy, who clearly wasn't an alpha, or apologizing into the air just in case Knox was listening in?

Except from the way he was looking at me, he was really talking to me.

Soft Smile sitting beside Nice Guy must have seen my confusion because she leaned in front of Nice Guy and said, "You're mated to one of our alphas. It's respectful—" She shot a stern look at everyone else "—to call the alpha's mate alpha as well, especially when apologizing or acknowledging a command."

Dear, God! They couldn't call me alpha. Cyrus would lose his mind.

He'd already made it crystal clear that I was not and

never would be an alpha in his pack. Surely this would push him over the edge and the punishment that I knew he was holding onto would happen. This was the kind of situation Merrick had loved: an impossible one that I had no control over.

The black-haired girl and Not-Velora shared a glance, something dark passing between them that they clearly wanted me to see. These shifters were able to communicate telepathically in their human forms unlike most shifters in my realm and they could have easily had a conversation without looking at each other.

"You're right, Quinn," the powerful girl in the group of four said. "Just because Knox is more reclusive than our other alphas doesn't mean he isn't one."

"My uncle also believes, given how Knox stays away from everyone and how powerful his reaction to his mate being hurt was that they have to be fated," Shy Girl said, offering me another tentative smile.

I returned it while everyone else stared at me again. Those in Nasty looked skeptical, everyone in Neutral was curious and nodded their agreement, while Nice Guy and the girl beside him, Quinn, looked happy and slightly amazed... because as I'd learned at dinner the other night, fated mates were just as rare here as they were back home.

Then Nova strode into the room, looked at me right away, and smiled. The tension that I'd been trying to ignore since Cyrus left me alone with strangers, eased a little, and Quinn blew out a soft breath as if she'd been tense, too.

"Sorry I'm late," Nova said as she shut the door behind her and set a bright yellow duffle bag in front of an empty chair between Nasty and Neutral. "Have you introduced yourselves to Audrey?"

AUDREY

THE MEMBERS OF THE NASTY GROUP started to nod their heads yes, claiming they'd already introduced themselves to me, when Nice Guy spoke up.

"We haven't. I'm Zavier. We were introduced a few days ago but you were pretty tired at the time and I don't expect you to remember."

Quinn introduced herself next, then the members of Neutral, and finally Nasty. The Neutral group did consist of two mated pairs, while the suspected siblings in Nasty were indeed siblings — twins in fact — and Not-Velora was Velora's younger sister.

After that, Nova started the class, pulling things out of the bright yellow bag and explaining what they were and how to use them. Then she started going into more detail about situations and the appropriate first aid.

My head was full by the time we stopped, two breaks and however many hours later — and from the angle of the sun shining through the large window at the back of the room, it had been at least five, probably six hours.

"That's it, everyone," Nova said. "If you feel overwhelmed, I'm more than happy to answer additional questions at any time, or you can sign up to take the class again."

"This is my second time," Zavier said to me.

"Of course it is," Not-Velora, aka Danica, scoffed as she strode out of the room, the rest of Nasty following her and laughing.

Zavier sighed and shot Quinn an exasperated look.

"Some people never outgrow school," Shy Girl, Hazel, said with a sad smile.

Her mate, the big bulky guy named Micah, hugged her against his side and pressed his lips against her temple. "It gets better."

"Yeah," Nova said with a wicked grin. "Now Zavier can give them citations."

"Probably not the smartest move to constantly cite Danica or the twins. They've both got family members in high places and don't mind being vindictive," Quinn replied.

"Spoilsport," Nova said with an exaggerated pout as she put all the medical supplies back into the duffle bag. "

The Neutral group said goodbye to all of us and left, and Nova hefted the bag over her shoulder.

"I think this calls for dinner and drinks," she said, glancing at me before turning to Quinn. "We haven't had a girls' night for over a month."

Zavier expelled an exaggerated sigh. "Guess it's back to my apartment for soup and water."

Quinn and Nova burst out laughing and rolled their eyes at him as if this was a common situation for them.

"I'm sure Nova will make an exception for you," Quinn assured him.

"Only because if we have a watchman with us, people will be less likely to corner Audrey." Nova turned to me. "What do you say?"

I wasn't sure what to say. Bishop had told me yesterday that he'd walk me to the community center and pick me up when the class was done, but he hadn't been able to get away from work to escort me and I had no idea if he was on his way right now or still tied up with Velora, a thought that made my mouth sour.

"Did I hear drinks?" Bishop asked as he walked through the door, startling me.

He rounded the table without hesitation, wrapped me into a fierce hug, and kissed me full on the lips, not caring who was in the room and what gossip he might be spreading.

I bit back a sigh. Was there any point in fighting it? Everyone would see it — or hear about it — by the end of tomorrow. Trying to keep it on the down-low was pointless.

Of course, after the looks from Danica and the rest of her group, I wasn't sure I wanted every woman in town to know that Bishop had decided I was going to be his mate.

It was bad enough when they just suspected something was going on between me and Cyrus. I wasn't prepared for every woman in the pack to outwardly hate me... which meant, as much as I didn't want to, I had to turn down Bishop's invitation to go to the festival.

I hadn't expected to be welcomed with open arms by the pack. I thought they'd be curious but respectful. But after the disastrous dinner with Cyrus and the betas, and the chilling welcome in class, I had serious doubts that they'd leave me alone.

Nova chuckled, flashing Bishop a genuine smile. "It never fails. Mention getting together and Bishop will suddenly show up."

"Hey!" he said with feigned shock. "I'm the social connection between the alphas and the pack. It's my duty to connect with everyone so Cyrus isn't forced to."

Zavier snorted and held out his hand to Quinn. "Looks like I win."

Quinn sighed, pulled out a few coins from her handbag, and handed them over. "Just because you're right, doesn't mean I'm wrong."

"About what?" Nova asked and Quinn's face turned bright red.

"I told her something was going on between you guys," Zavier said, pointing to me and Bishop. "But little miss here"— He jerked his thumb toward Quinn. "She said there hadn't been rumors about Cyrus and anyone for a few years and they started again when Audrey showed up. That had to mean something."

I bit back a groan. "There's nothing between me and Cyrus."

"Oh, there's something," Zavier said as we headed out of the room and down the hall. "He personally escorted you here and then checked the room for danger."

"He was looking for Nova," I insisted. "Trust me. Cyrus doesn't like me." Not as a friend or a family member and especially not romantically like they were insisting.

"Sorry, Audrey," Quinn replied. "He definitely checked the room for danger before he left."

"Because I'm mated to his brother."

God, I really hoped no one else in the class thought Cyrus had checked out the room to ensure I was safe before he left. Because he hadn't. He never would.

He'd been stiff and angry the whole walk down here, a clear sign that he didn't enjoy my company. But of course, no one believed me. My word was never good enough.

"Tell them," I said, looking up at Bishop as we left the community center and headed down the street.

He had his arm across my shoulders and was possessively holding me to his side. The heat of our shifter connection warmed around my heart and I relaxed into him despite my worry that being seen with him was going to cause trouble.

If he was with me, I was safe. I'd always be safe.

"Where are we grabbing dinner?" Bishop asked, not answering my question.

"Annalise's," Nova replied. "It's halfway between here and the Residence and has a mostly hidden patio. I suspect Audrey would prefer someplace quiet and not in the main square."

"The main square's too nosy to have a decent conversation anyway," Zavier agreed, although I suspected Nova had made the suggestion so I wouldn't get swarmed by people curious about the stranger who'd mated Knox and was getting far too cozy with Bishop, and I greatly appreciated it.

We wound our way up narrow streets, avoiding the main road, until we reached a three-story building a block from the towering Old Town wall. It was a triangular structure placed on a small terrace between larger ones above and below it, and a sign hung above a bright blue door announcing the business in a strange flowing script that I couldn't read, reminding me I still needed to learn.

Zavier opened the door and a gust of mouthwatering smells washed over us as we stepped into a small dining room with a dozen tables, half of which were occupied. A few of the diners glanced up to see who'd entered then did a double take, staring at me and Bishop.

By the time we'd reached the side door near the back of the dining room, everyone was staring, making my insides twist. I could see the curiosity and judgment in their eyes and wanted to beg Bishop to take me back to the Residence so I could hide in my suite.

I wasn't ready for this kind of attention. I didn't think

I'd ever be ready, especially when I knew my position in the pack was precarious.

"Unbelievable," Zavier hissed as he opened the door, revealing three narrow steps leading up to the patio.

"They'll come around. They're just curious," Nova said, climbing the steps to a magical patio, or rather, a secret courtyard.

Buildings surrounded it, the rise of the land dictating their placement and shape, creating the hidden space. In the center stood an enormous tree, its branches spread wide, creating a leafy canopy over the entire area with wisteria and this realm's version of fairy lights hanging from the branches.

With the shade from the tree and the growing shadow of the mountain creeping over the town as the sun inched toward setting, I could see a hint of soft light emanating from the magical light stones and could just imagine how beautiful everything would look after sunset.

"Wow," I gasped and Quinn grinned at me.

"That's what I thought the first time I came here. I'm glad Nova picked this place."

"And only one set of nosy diners to contend with," Zavier huffed, shooting a glare at a couple sitting in a cozy corner created by the front of the restaurant and its neighboring building. "I mean, I get the girls. They all wanted to be Bishop's mate and now it's obvious he's off the market."

Quinn gave him a playful shove. "Not everyone wants to be Bishop's mate."

"Ouch," Bishop gasped, pressing a hand over his heart in exaggerated pain. "You don't want me, Quinn?"

She rolled her eyes at him. "I'm sure you'll survive."

"You bet I will," he replied, hugging me close to his side. "I've found my life's mate. There are no other women in the world."

Warmth shot through my chest at his words. I was his life's mate. He'd actually said it in front of Nova, Zavier, and Quinn. Not that I'd expected him to hide our relationship, but the only person who'd publicly declared he wanted me was Royce and that had been a trick.

"Come on, let's sit over here. They won't be able to stare through the *throver* tree." Bishop tugged me to the back of the patio to a four-person table, pulled out a chair for me, then grabbed a chair from a nearby table and sat beside me.

After we'd all settled and a waiter had come to tell us the four things the chef was cooking that night, we ate and talked and laughed.

The tension that had been coiled inside me about how people were going to treat me melted away like it always did when I was around Bishop and the few others I trusted. And Quinn and Zavier quickly joined that group. They didn't ask me questions, although I was sure they were curious about everything. They just treated me like a normal person.

The feeling was strange, but also incredible.

Maybe I could find a place in this pack other than just being Knox's or Bishop's mate. It didn't feel as if Quinn and Zavier were being nice to me because of Bishop. It felt like they liked me for me, like how Eloise and Kira made me feel.

I could live with that. Four possible friends were three more than I had in my old pack. I also had Knox and Bishop as well as Nova, Deacon, and Whil. I could happily be content with a quiet life if I had this.

Warmth radiated around my heart and for a second it felt as if my soul was creating a shifter connection with everyone at the table and not just Bishop even though we weren't in close contact. I might not have known the others as well as Bishop, but something in my soul assured me I was safe with them.

Which was crazy. I barely knew them. That, and that thing inside me was also certain that I was safe with Cyrus, which made me seriously doubt my certainty.

Except right in this moment I didn't want to. Sitting with them on the patio felt too good. It was a glimpse of what might be possible and I never wanted to let it go.

As I savored the strange feeling of peace and laughed softly at Bishop and Zavier's bad jokes, and Nova and Quinn's eye rolls, a new sensation seeped into me.

It was urgent and needy, an overwhelming desire to get somewhere. Faster, faster!

But I didn't know where and I didn't know what I was suddenly desperate about or why.

I forced a smile and nodded at something Quinn said, although I didn't fully hear her. She taught the younger kids at the school and was in the middle of telling a story about their adorable antics. I was also sure she had horror stories about them misbehaving, but so far, she hadn't mentioned any of them.

Nova added something and Bishop and Zavier burst out laughing. I forced my smile brighter but didn't try to fake a laugh. I wasn't that good of an actress and they'd see right through me. Better to stay quiet and avoid drawing attention to myself.

Except Bishop still noticed something wasn't right.

"Audrey?" he asked, his voice filled with concern.

"I'm fine." I tried to make my smile more convincing, but that only made him frown and everyone else look at me with concern.

"What are you feeling?" Nova asked. "Was it something from the meal? So far, you've been able to eat and drink everything in this realm, but we can't assume that will always be the case."

"That's not it." I pressed a hand over my heart, the urgency squeezing tighter.

Faster. Faster. Soon soon soon.

Soon it would be right, the way it was supposed to be, the way it should always be.

AUDREY

A MOMENT LATER, THE PRESSURE EXPLODED INTO RELIEF, and a soul-deep love flooded into every cell in my body.

"Knox," I breathed, joy rushing up inside me to match his love. "Knox is back."

Zavier frowned. "He told you?"

"No." I turned to see his enormous black wolf mostly hidden in the shadows of an alley between the neighboring buildings. I doubted I'd have been able to see him if I hadn't just known exactly where to look.

Audrey, he rumbled in my head, and before I realized what I was doing, I raced across the courtyard and threw myself at him.

He shifted into his human form in the blink of an eye and caught me mid-leap in a crushing embrace.

Our mouths crashed together in a hungry kiss, igniting our desires since our desires fed off each other in a never-ending loop. An emptiness in my soul that I hadn't fully realized was there but had sunk into my essence the moment I'd stopped feeling Knox's emotions melted away.

"I missed you," he said, his voice low as he pulled me up, clutching me tighter.

Instinctively, I wrapped my legs around his waist, my hot core pressed against his hardening cock. With a groan, he pinned me against the alley wall. His fingers tangled into my hair and he jerked my head back and deepened our kiss with a ferocity that matched my dream-Knox.

"Sisters, I missed you," he gasped, suddenly breaking the kiss and pressing his forehead against mine.

Our breathing had turned ragged and desire zinged through our bond, but I could also feel him trying to get a hold of himself. He'd made a promise to not have sex with me until I'd forgiven him for hurting me when he'd refused our bond.

But for the life of me, I couldn't understand why I'd been so determined to put off our fate. I wanted him more than I wanted my next breath, and I'd been numb and aching without even realizing it while he'd been gone.

"I missed you, too," I replied, sliding my hands down his naked, sculpted chest to his cock trapped between us. It was already thick and hard and leaking precum, and I wanted nothing more than to have him buried inside me.

Someone cleared his throat and I jerked my gaze to Bishop and the others at the table. They were watching us with a mix of emotions. Bishop had a wicked grin as if he were getting pleasure out of Knox working me up, the thought sending more desire spiraling to my core, and Nova looked happy while Quinn and Zavier were in complete shock.

"Well, if there was any doubt about them being mated..." Zavier said. "I'd say that clears that up."

Quinn slapped him on the arm. "There never was any doubt and you should be happy for them."

A flicker of unease seeped through my mating bond and Knox's gaze darted around the courtyard as if he suddenly realized we were out in public. When he saw the only people were us — the other couple having left a while ago — the unease vanished even though his grip on me tightened.

"We're leaving," he announced, quickly turning on his heel and carrying me down the alley, before I had a chance to say goodbye.

But in that moment, I didn't care. I felt the same urgency he did, the need to re-consummate our bond again and again.

At the end of the alley, Knox shifted back to his wolf and I climbed on top and clung to him as he raced along mostly deserted back streets and alleys back to the Residence. Without slowing, he rushed through the open gate and skirted the Residence's tall wall, heading away from the castle and deep into the grounds.

He bounded over flowerbeds and bushes and leaped up hills, his powerful muscles bunching beneath me, his soft fur caressing my neck and chin as I clung to him, and his seductive wood smoke scent wrapping around me.

The air rushed through my hair and swept cool over my face, easing the summer heat as we ran. Joy surged through our bond, Knox's feeling of freedom and power flowing into me and filling me up with sensations I'd never felt before.

I whooped with joy, feeling wild as if the world was filled with amazing sights and sounds and opportunities and they were all at my fingertips.

The wildness flooded my body and my next whoop turned into a human howl of thanks to the moons, the Two Sisters of the Night.

Knox joined my howl and we bounded up a narrow path cut into a stony ridge at the back of the Residence's grounds up to a wide ledge that overlooked the town.

I slid off his back, awed at the view. Warm, inviting lights shone through the windows and in what I could only assume were public gathering areas since I hadn't been in that part of the city after dark. From this distance, they sparkled like stars, a property of the magic that made them glow.

Beyond, to my left and past another part of town I'd yet to see, stood a vast forest that climbed up into the mountains. That had to be where the pack's sacred grove was since the small one on the Residence's grounds was only big enough for a handful of people, not the whole town. Above me, stars filled the night sky, bright against the darkness even though the Sisters looked almost full.

Behind me, Knox shifted and drew me down to the ground so we could cuddle together while stargazing.

"It's beautiful," I whispered as if speaking too loudly would shatter the magical stillness enveloping us.

"This is my favorite spot on the grounds," Knox replied. "When the weather's good, I sleep up here. Not that I expect you to— I mean, I wouldn't—"

I nuzzled closer to him, taking in deep breaths of his scent, and placed my palm over his heart hyperaware that he was completely naked and I was still a little worked up. "I know what you mean. You wanted to share this with me."

"I've been thinking about bringing you here since the night I left."

Contentment and peace radiated through our bond, and a giggle bubbled up inside me from the joy and awe and love, things I'd never expected to feel. Everything in my being said this was where I was supposed to be, and tonight I wasn't going to question it or fight it. I'd never seen Knox so calm before, so at ease, but he was finally in his element with just the two of us in nature, and he'd fully accepted our bond.

"I couldn't stop thinking of you and I felt so empty," he said, tightening his grip around me and pressing his lips to my forehead. "Will you let me hold you?"

I raised my head until our lips met. Knox hadn't outwardly begged a whole lot, but I could feel it through our bond how truly sorry he was for hurting me, which was all I really needed to know. "I'd like it if you did more than hold me."

"But I promised—" I brushed my lips against his and his breath hitched. "I haven't begged enough. You swore—"

"And I've changed my mind. I missed you, too." I slid my hand over the sculpted contours of his chest. "I need you, Knox,"

Without hesitation, he captured my lips in a hungry kiss, surprise and awe rushing through the bond before being consumed with desire.

I kissed him back, just as hungry. I hadn't thought I'd give in so easily, but the mating bond was a powerful magic and connected us in a way we'd never been connected before.

I *knew* he didn't want to hold back or deny me, and I *knew* he wouldn't use this moment to hurt me.

It seemed foolish to change my mind so quickly, but the bond reassured me. Now that we'd sealed it and Knox had accepted it, I was safe with him, body, heart, and soul.

I tangled my fingers in his hair, holding him close, never wanting to let him go. With a groan, he ground his cock into the crux of my leg between my thigh and mound.

Anticipation shivered down my spine. I felt as if I'd been waiting for this all my life. I didn't fully remember the first time we'd joined. I'd been partially delirious from the heat fever. But this time would be seared into my memory. And if intercourse with Knox was anything like when he went down on me, it was going to be amazing.

He groaned again and shoved one hand under my shirt and roughly palmed my breasts. I arched into his touch, my body begging for more, knowing this wasn't going to be a gentle lovemaking. I could already feel the frenzy building inside him and his struggle to hold himself back.

"Knox, it's—"

A flash of brilliant light lit up the night sky followed by an explosive clap of thunder.

"Fu—" Knox snarled.

But before he could even finish the word, rain crashed over us in a warm torrential downpour.

I gasped at the sudden assault, my hair and clothes instantly soaked by the storm that hadn't been there a moment ago.

Knox pulled me into his arms and stood.

"What's going on?" I asked, trying to wipe water from my eyes, disappointment that we'd been interrupted souring my desire. I'd been more than ready to be with him, to join our bodies like our souls were joined, and now the moment was gone.

"It's the rainy season." He hurried off the ledge and down the uneven path to the ground. "In the summer the wind changes and the storms that roll off two of the storm gods' resting places in the south are more likely to hit us. That's why they come out of nowhere and are so powerful."

He reached the bottom and sprinted across the Residence's ground, his wolf rising to the surface and a wildness rushing through our bond.

It was the same wildness I'd felt when riding him, primal, fierce, joyful. It didn't matter that it was raining and we could barely see more than a few feet away from us. The power in the storm called to the beast within him.

And through him, I could almost imagine my own wolf rising up, riding on the energy sparking and flashing in the force of nature pouring down on us.

Thunder clapped again, sharp and explosive, rattling my bones and filling me up. With Knox's emotions riding me, I felt powerful, unstoppable. I wanted to run, too. But in reality, I'd just slow him down.

"Run with me," he— no his wolf said as if he could read my mind — and with our emotions so strongly connected maybe he could. "I know you can feel it. The power crackling all around us."

As if to punctuate his words, lightning flashed and thunder clapped again.

"Run, Audrey. Run with me."

He set me on the ground, grabbed my hand, and I had no choice but to run or be dragged behind him.

I raced as fast as I could with Knox keeping pace at my side, sprinting around trees, shrubs, and flowerbeds, the wind whipping warm rain in my face.

Exhilaration welled up inside me fed by Knox's wild joy, and once again, I howled, letting the storm devour my voice.

I hadn't liked running before, but then I'd been running to escape and stay safe. This was completely different. Just like when I'd ridden Knox, I felt free. I felt like a part of me did contain a wild wolf and by running for joy, I was letting a little piece of her out.

We rounded a small copse of trees and there in the distance through the downpour was the soft warm glow of shelter.

The light wasn't very bright, perhaps just a lamp in someone's window. Whatever it was, it only made Knox happier, which confused me. If I went inside, this amazing moment would end, and I never wanted it to end.

But a few seconds later, I realized the light wasn't coming from the Residence. It came from Whil's cottage greenhouse, the shimmering glass orb by her front door that I'd originally assumed was a whimsical decoration but was actually a light.

"In here," Knox said, guiding me to the greenhouse door.

Gasping, I hurried inside, water rushing off me into a large puddle on the uneven flagstone floor.

"That was—" I sucked in rapid breaths filled with the sweet scent of Whil's flowers and the rich wood smoke that was all Knox.

Exhilaration still raced through my veins, even

though I was out of breath, more powerful than our run to the ledge. And mixed within it, was Knox's joy.

I met his wild grin, his canines extended and his eyes dark, and the exhilaration turned hot. His gaze raked down my body with so much heat my whole body was aching and strung tight with desire by the time he looked back up again.

"Mine," he snarled.

"Yes," I gasped back and we crashed together, our lips meeting in a frenzied kiss.

KNOX

I KISSED AUDREY WITH A HUNGER I'D NEVER KNOWN before, a hunger that had been growing the moment I'd tasted her the other night and hadn't been satisfied because I'd had to go on that fucking hunt.

Not that I hadn't loved the thrill of the chase and the peacefulness of being alone, but I needed Audrey more. And if it came down to it, I'd give up hunting for Audrey. I'd give up all of it.

Of course, she'd never ask that of me, even if it was to her own detriment. I was a complete idiot for thinking she'd trap me. I was the one trapping her. She was stuck with a mate who couldn't give her everything.

"Whatever you're thinking," she said, grabbing a handful of my hair and yanking it to catch my attention. "Stop it. It's not true and I need you, Knox. Now. Please."

A whine edged her tone and the force of her need swelled through our bond, consuming my doubts and insecurities while my wolf snarled at me for being stupid. I had our gorgeous, fragile mate in our arms and she ached for us. Just like I ached for her and had been for the last four days.

"Mine," my wolf snarled, itching to be the one to claim her this time.

He seized control of our body, jerked her head back by her hair, and kissed her like he was starving.

He'd told me from the beginning that Audrey was ours and I'd resisted much to his growing fury. I also hadn't let him take over when we'd sealed the bond because of her fragile state from her heat, and he was still angry about that, too.

Audrey moaned into my mouth, leaning into my embrace. Her wet clothes dragged against my naked flesh. Her hard nipples, straining against the practically see-through fabric, drew short erotic lines against my chest with every quick breath, while the rougher fabric of her pants ground against my straining cock.

Fuck. I wanted nothing more than to give in to my wolf and bury myself into her tight, slick heat. One powerful stroke and I'd be where I was supposed to be.

But Bishop had warned me before I'd left for the hunt to make sure she was ready first. Sure, she wasn't a virgin anymore and had had marathon sex during her heat, but she was still inexperienced. I couldn't let go like I had in our shared dreams when we'd first been bound together no matter what my wolf wanted.

But it was getting harder and harder to think straight with her need pouring through our mating bond.

Sisters, I needed to get my mouth on her and taste the liquid desire leaking from her pussy and perfuming the air with her seductive, sweet scent.

"Too many clothes," my wolf said, grabbing the front of her shirt and tearing it open.

Audrey's breath hitched and a blast of her need shot painfully to my cock.

Fuck me. I was going to take her right on the cold wet flagstones if I didn't do something about it. Now.

Struggling against my wolf, I picked her up and carried her the few feet to one of Whil's reading nooks. It lay in a pop-out section in the greenhouse's wall with two fully glassed walls and two waist-high walls, leaving the space open to the rest of the greenhouse. With its all-glass ceiling and only minimum foliage to block the outside, the space didn't set off my claustrophobia as quickly as other spaces. I still couldn't spend the whole night, but I could satisfy Audrey a few times before I had to get back outside.

I tossed her onto the slightly raised, cushioned floor, watching her pert tits bounce and her mouth open in a surprised "oh."

And now all I could think about were her perfect lips wrapped around my cock.

But not now. Later. Gods damned later.

She didn't remember much of her heat, so I was sure she didn't remember drinking Bishop down night after night and I wasn't going to remind her. She was shy enough about sex and I didn't want to risk her withdrawing from me.

Her half-lidded gaze raked over my body, slowly sliding down my chest to my cock, and she licked her lips.

Oh, Sisters!

Maybe I was wrong about what she remembered.

"You want this?" I asked, my voice barely more than a rumble as I grabbed my cock and squeezed the base, trying to calm the fuck down.

Her gaze dipped to my feet and a blush rushed over her cheeks and down her neck, straight to her taut nipples even as her desire in our bond burned hotter. It blazed around my heart before sinking into my throbbing groin, making me grit my teeth, desperate to stay in control.

"Do you want this?" I barked as I stepped onto the cushions.

A hint of alpha power snapped through my words, yanking her attention back to my cock. I slowly pumped up then back down my length, her attention riveted on my hand.

"Take me," I ordered, making sure to have a firm grip on my power, and was rewarded with another breathtaking blast of lust, mixed with a hint of uncertainty.

"I haven't done it—" She frowned as if she wasn't certain whether she'd sucked cock before, adding to my suspicion that she didn't remember much from her heat. "I won't be very good."

"Take me," my wolf growled again, this time with a sharp blast of power.

A whisper of her power, a power I'd been feeling since we'd run through the rain rose to meet me. It wasn't strong like it had been in our dreams or the first time I'd made her come after nearly dying, but I could still feel it. It was a swirling dancing promise, a siren's song to my own alpha power, and the truth of her soul that was hidden so deep it was almost impossible to recognize.

She rose to her knees, her breath becoming rapid gasps. In this position, her mouth was barely an inch from my cock.

"Audrey," I groaned, brushing myself against her bottom lip, leaving a glistening trail of precum.

Her tongue darted out, licking me up, and it was more than I could handle. With a growl, I grabbed a fistful of her hair and jerked hard. She gasped at the pain even as more desire flooded our bond and thickened the air, and I pushed my cock into her mouth.

"I'm going to fuck your mouth, Audrey," I snarled, my body trembling as I held myself back. "You want me to stop, you say so now, because once I start, I'm not stopping."

Not that I wouldn't stop if her emotions changed. But I also knew she wouldn't say no. She wanted this so much it hurt but she was afraid to ask for it.

I rocked my hips forward, a shallow thrust to get her started. "Last, chance."

Her eyes met mine and sucked me in deeper.

"Then hang on."

Her small hands wrapped around the back of my thighs and I withdrew from her wet heat and thrust back in again a little harder and deeper.

Her gaze never left mine, blazing with desire and fueling my need to claim every last inch of her. I firmly held her head where I wanted her and thrust again and again, making sure to keep on the right side of the edge of hard and fast.

She sucked and moaned, her desire pouring through me, urging me on, threatening what little control I had, and the air was thick with her arousal.

I hit the back of her throat, making her gag and sending arousal zinging through our bond.

"Relax," I snarled, angling her head back, pushing deeper, feeling her throat contract around my tip as she tried to swallow.

Fuck. Sex had never felt this good before. Even if I couldn't fuck her mouth fully, it was still the most incredible sensation. But then, I'd never had a direct emotional connection to a lover before.

Audrey liked a little roughness. She liked it when I took control. I just couldn't let it go to my head and push her past her limits. And I sure as hell couldn't blow my load down her throat. I wanted to come in her tight pussy, wanted to feel my seed filling her even though I knew she was on the birth inhibitor extract and I couldn't get her pregnant. Something primal inside me needed to fill her with my cum again and again and permanently mark her with my scent.

Fuck.

I yanked out of her mouth, making her whine at the loss, shoved her back against the cushions, and tore her pants from her body.

She gasped, shocked and turned on, and I buried my face between her thighs. She smelled incredible and was already dripping wet and desperate for me.

"Knox, please."

I lapped at her juices, flicking my tongue against her clit, once, twice, three times and she was crashing over the edge of ecstasy on a strangled moan.

More nectar gushed out of her — what Bishop had told me I needed to enter her — and I gripped her hips, lined up my cock, and plunged into her in a quick, powerful stroke just like I wanted. She moaned even louder, her walls fluttering around me, and her eyes rolled back in pleasure.

"Fuck me, Knox," she begged. "Fuck me hard."

I chuckled, knowing she'd be mortified in the morning that she'd said that and loving that I'd gotten her to fully relax around me and tell me what she wanted.

I fucked her until she was writhing and screaming, and the tingling up my spine and the pressure in my balls was almost too much to handle. But I still held it together, taking her over the edge again and tearing out a third climax before the second was even done.

"One more," I commanded, grinding my thumb against her clit and pumping fast and hard.

Her little tits bounced with each impact, the sound of flesh smacking flesh along with my moans and her screams filling the greenhouse. Sweat slicked her forehead and strands of her blond hair were stuck to her skin. She looked like a goddess, practically glowing with bliss and I never wanted it to stop.

"I can't," she gasped, shaking her head, even as her walls began to flutter, a precursor to her coming.

"You can. You will." My alpha power rose up, not in a command, but a challenge, and her power rose up to meet mine. It was barely there, but without a doubt, it was there. She *had* power, she just needed to realize it. It was a seductive, swirling glimmer that teased mine, wove itself through mine, and made my wolf howl, calling out to awaken the wolf half of his mate.

"Oh, God," she gasped, her body trembling, and my wolf howled again then completely took over.

I rode the building wave with him, reveling in the glorious sensation of our cock pounding into her, her body arching up to meet mine, thrust for thrust, and our pleasure feeding off each other.

More. More more more, my wolf growled, needing to feel her come again as much as I did.

"Come." My power rushed over her and her muscles contracted, tearing my own orgasm free. I howled with my pleasure as well as hers, a wild loop of sensation rushing through our bond as my hot cum streamed into her and our bodies locked in a primal battle of life and love.

Fate had been cruel to me in the past, trapping me for days, crushed under heavy rock in complete darkness, but I wouldn't change any of it if it meant I could keep Audrey. She was an amazing gift, one I hadn't known I wanted and certainly didn't deserve.

She was the other half of my dual soul, a perfect match to both human and wolf. I'd always been meant for her and I'd be by her side, protecting and loving her forever. The way it was always supposed to be.

AUDREY

I woke to soft kisses against my jaw and a growing sense of unease, even as warmth and affection flowed through our mating bond.

"You have to go," I mumbled, understanding that he couldn't stay inside any longer but still disappointed that he wasn't waking me up for more sex like he had the last time.

Of course, after the hard sex at the beginning of the night and the slower, drawn-out lovemaking when the Sisters were high in the sky, I wasn't sure my body could handle another round.

I wasn't even sure I'd be able to walk normally and not give away the fact I'd had mind-blowing sex with my mate... not that I needed to hide that, but too many people were looking at me as it was and I didn't want to give them more to talk about.

"I do," he rumbled, his warm breath feathering across my cheek as he tightened his grip around me.

I snuggled back against his chest and breathed in his rich wood smoke scent, not ready to open my eyes and watch him leave.

I wanted to stay in Whil's greenhouse forever, lying on the soft mattress covering the floor, warmed by the hot stone in a metal bowl, covered by a light sheet, and wrapped in his arms.

"I don't want you to go."

"Neither do I, but I—" Fear blossomed in our bond and I sent my love back to combat it. And somehow, even though I didn't fully know him yet, I really did love him.

"I understand," I told him. "It's alright."

Reluctantly, I cracked open my eyes, surprised to see the sky lightening and an early morning mist clinging to the gardens beyond the glass.

"You stayed the night," I gasped, rolling to face him.

"You steady my soul." He brushed his lips against mine in a tender kiss. "I can last longer in Whil's greenhouse than any other structure, but usually not more than five or so hours."

I kissed him back with more heat. "Thank you for staying the night."

"I'd stay every night with you if I could. But Whil won't agree to that."

I cringed, heat spreading across my face. I hadn't been quiet during our lovemaking, had just let go for once, too caught up in the moment. Whil had to have heard everything—

Oh my God! She had to have heard me beg Knox to fuck me harder.

My hot face turned into an inferno with embarrassment and to top it off, Knox had torn my clothes to shreds and I was going to have to do the walk of shame back to my suite in a sheet.

Except it wasn't a walk of shame. Knox and I were bonded mates. We were expected to have sex, a lot of sex, especially in the beginning when we were still getting used to the bond.

Then a new thought struck me. "Is it just Whil's greenhouse that gives you extra time indoors or all greenhouses?"

"A couple of our farmers have greenhouses," he said with a chuckle, probably laughing at the color of my face. "But I've never stayed longer than an hour in any of them."

"But could you stay longer if you had the chance?" I asked, shocked at how simple the solution was for us being together. If, of course, I could get over the fact that anyone could walk by and see us having sex.

Maybe getting the pack engineers to figure out one-way glass was my first priority. Except I had no idea what went into making one-way glass. And, on top of that, it would have to work with the lights being off *and* on, and I didn't know if even the glass in my realm could handle that or if Knox could even withstand the tinted glass like he could the regular glass.

Maybe it would be better just building a very tall garden and hope for the best. But if the pack was talking about me now, someone would surely jump at the chance to watch me and Knox going at it. Probably a lot of someones.

"We need to go up!" I gasped.

Knox huffed even as his lips quirked in a barely-there smile. "What are you talking about?"

"Building us a greenhouse." I turned my attention to the Residence's towers peeking out between the trees. "Is there access to the Residence's roof?"

But as soon as I asked that, my excitement soured. It didn't matter if we could build on the Residence's roof or not. It would cost money and I'd need Cyrus's permission. He could easily deny me as a way of reminding me of my place. Knox had been getting along just fine without a greenhouse bedroom, and I, as a weak shifter, was supposed to accept my alpha's and mate's way of life. It didn't matter that I couldn't shift and was more vulnerable to the elements.

"Audrey," Knox growled, dragging my attention away from the ruins of a possible great plan. "It's a good idea."

"But it's too much. I haven't shown anyone that I deserve it."

"What the fuck are you talking about?" he snapped.

I jumped at the sharpness in his voice and instinctively started to make myself smaller even though the action frustrated me and I knew Knox wouldn't hurt me.

"Shit." Panic swept through the bond and he cupped my face in his large palms. "I'm sorry. I didn't mean to snap. I'm not angry with you."

"I know," I replied, my voice frustratingly small. I nuzzled against his neck, seeking comfort from him to steady my soul. "It's a habit. I can't seem to break it even when I'm around you."

Probably because I couldn't break it around Cyrus and the majority of the pack.

"Bishop would say it just takes time," Knox huffed. "But I'm still waiting."

The unease radiating through the bond increased and he growled in frustration.

"Go," I told him, not wanting to be the reason he was torturing himself. "I'll be okay."

"Bishop is on his way with breakfast and clothes. I'll stick around until he shows up, then I have to report to Deacon about the hunt." He rolled away from me, got up, and strode out of the greenhouse as if he couldn't stop for a second.

I gathered the sheet around me, tapped the side of the heating bowl to deactivate the hot stone, and followed him outside.

"What are you doing?" he asked before shifting into his wolf form, all the stress and discomfort from being inside melting away as he gave into his wolf nature.

"If you're sticking around, we might as well sit together." I sat on the shallow step in front of the greenhouse's door and Knox settled beside me, a furry heater that smelled like love and safety and home.

Knox rumbled, the sound vibrating through my body, relaxing me even more, and just like our desire, our contentment fed off each other, making me feel, just for a moment, as if I were completely safe and had the space to figure out who I was.

I didn't want the feeling to end, but I knew it would the moment Knox left. "Will you come back after talking with Deacon?"

"Until you and Bishop leave for the festival," he assured me, reminding me of how nervous I was to go to the festival and how excited Bishop was to show me.

But it was bittersweet because Knox couldn't join us.

I quickly shoved that emotion back and focused on my excitement. I didn't want Knox to feel guilty about not being able to come to the festival with me. I'd promised I'd accept all of him and I would. We would have our own special moments together. Perhaps, once I'd proven my usefulness to Cyrus, we'd have them in a greenhouse bedroom where he could stay the whole night.

AUDREY

Bishop arrived a few minutes later with clothes and breakfast and Knox left to report about his hunt to Deacon. We ate and chatted, Bishop's excitement about the festival bubbling out of him.

A part of me wanted to tell him I'd changed my mind about going. When I'd agreed, I hadn't known how everyone would judge me like the nasty group in the first aid class or stare at me like they had last night in the restaurant. I didn't want to face more people like that and from the way Bishop was talking about it, most of the pack visited the festival all five days. It was going to be busy.

Except if I refused to go because I didn't want everyone looking at me, then I'd be stuck hiding in the Residence for who knew how long, a self-made prisoner. And I really didn't want that.

I wanted to go out with Bishop not just to the festival

but to do other things. Kira had invited me to the restaurant where she was learning new dishes and I wanted to taste them.

If I could get through having everyone stare at me at the festival, most of the pack would learn in one fell swoop that I was plain and boring and a weakling. I wasn't a threat like Finn and Velora believed... although from the way I'd caught Velora looking at Bishop maybe I was a threat to her.

On top of that, Bishop would be with me the entire time. I had no doubt that he'd keep me safe. All I needed to do was stay close, put up with the stares and the whispered comments, and hopefully soon after that, they'd forget about how interesting I was. I wouldn't be able to leave the Residence by myself. That was just calling for trouble, but I'd hopefully be able to enjoy future outings.

A couple of hours after I'd convinced myself it was better to go than to stay hiding in the Residence, Knox returned. The three of us chatted some more until it was just before lunch.

We left Knox and returned to my suite so I could have a quick shower. That turned into a longer shower when Bishop offered to wash me and we'd ended up teasing each other with hands and lips, but thankfully didn't go beyond that since I really was sore from last night.

It also didn't feel weird like I was afraid it would. I wasn't uncomfortable knowing I'd had sex with Knox and the next day was making out in the shower with Bishop.

And it was a great distraction from my nerves about the festival.

I wanted to feel feminine and beautiful for Bishop since this was an official courting date, but I didn't want everyone staring at all my scars so I ended up wearing a green shirt that matched the flecks in Bishop's eyes and a pair of light, loose, beige pants.

Then we headed to the festival, strolling down the streets while I made an effort to not make eye contact with anyone so I wouldn't see them staring at me.

From the way the road sloped, I saw the festival before we reached it, the sight stealing my breath for a second. Even from a distance, I could tell there were going to be hundreds of things to see and do because it looked like the market on steroids.

It had at least a hundred more tents and stalls than the market I'd seen before, so many that they poured past the boundaries of Stonehaven onto the grassy plains. Flags and banners fluttered in the summer breeze, adding to the cacophony of colors from the tents and people, some wearing bright colors and others with flower crowns and necklaces, and— Oh! There were more overflowing planter boxes where there hadn't been before filled with flowers.

As we drew closer, the wind shifted, carrying a mouth-watering mix of aromas, and the voices from all the people grew louder.

I inched closer to Bishop, uneasy about stepping into the crowd with the pack's most eligible bachelor.

Maybe this was a bad idea after all.

I could already guess what everyone would think about me. The nasty group at the first aid class had made it perfectly clear.

Although not everyone had thought that. The neutral group had been curious, not judging, and Quinn and Zavier had been friendly and inviting. All I really needed to worry about was not embarrassing myself or drawing more attention than I already was and giving Cyrus or his betas more reasons to be mad at me.

We reached the crowd and those closest to us went silent.

Oh, crap.

My pulse lurched and I locked my gaze on the road just ahead of my toes. Everyone was looking at me.

"Look up, Audrey," Bishop murmured, his voice so low I could barely hear him. "You've got this."

I swallowed hard. I couldn't spend my life hiding in the Residence from the pack. Even if I could, I'd still have to hide because Velora and Finn didn't like me. I had to do this.

I *could* do this.

I raised my gaze and tried to smile but couldn't stop feeling like I was a strange specimen on display.

"Everyone. This is Audrey," Bishop announced and those farther down the street quieted and looked in our direction.

I tried to breathe through my rising panic. I didn't

want to be there, didn't want people looking at me, judging me, seeing everything that was wrong with me.

People glanced at each other, a few said something, their mouths moving, but I wasn't close enough to hear them.

Were they wondering what I was doing with Bishop?

Of course they were. I was Knox's mate. I was supposed to stay in my lane and hide from the rest of the pack with Knox.

And boy, right now, I wanted to hide.

Stop looking at me, I mentally begged. *Go back to what you were doing. Please.*

This was a mistake, a horrible, terrible mistake. I shouldn't be here, shouldn't have left the Residence. But that would mean I was trapped for life and I couldn't accept that.

Except could I accept all these people staring at me?

I glanced at Bishop who was beaming at me as if he were oblivious to the awkward silence, and warmth from our shifter connection warmed around my heart.

Yes. Yes, I could. People were always going to stare at me. I was just going to have to live with that. But really, most people wouldn't care what I did or who I was with. I was merely today's curiosity and tomorrow's gossip. After that, I'd just be Audrey.

I drew in a slow breath and squared my shoulders.

I'd faced monsters and survived. I could face normal, everyday shifters.

"Someone needs some flowers," a woman with a

basket of flowers said, breaking the awkward moment and everyone else burst back into action as if they'd been frozen in the moment just like me.

"Bishop, you're losing your game," another man called out making those around him laugh.

A few more people started ribbing Bishop while others laughed, and while I could see there were still a lot of people staring at me with a mix of negative expressions varying from concern to disgust and outright hate, there were those, now that the shock of the moment was gone, who were a mix of curious or friendly.

See, it isn't everyone. And a few was a lot better than none. Maybe I could have a place in this pack.

"You're Knox's mate," a teenaged girl said as she held out a crown made of bright yellow flowers.

"I am. I'm sorry," I replied, looking at the flower crown. "I don't have any money."

"Don't be silly." She reached up and put it on my head then her expression turned sad. "Mom and I heard you're from far away and all by yourself. We made this one special for you to welcome you to the pack."

My throat tightened and tears pricked my eyes.

"My mom also says—" She glanced at Bishop before looking back at me and sighing the kind of sigh girls in the movies sighed when they fell in love "—that you and Knox are fated, which probably means you and Bishop are fated because they're twins and all. It's just so romantic."

The woman with the basket pushed past a couple of

men still teasing Bishop and tugged on the girl's arm. "Welcome to the pack, alpha."

My pulse lurched. Was everyone going to call me that?

"Come on, Everly, before those old men rope the alpha into something he can't get away from. I'm sure these two want to enjoy the festival." The woman gave me a warm, welcoming smile and not-so-accidentally bumped into the man beside her. "Donovan, have you gotten your wife a flower crown yet?"

"No," he replied.

"Then you should pick one now before all the good ones are gone." She gave me a wink and nudged the other two guys talking with Bishop.

Bishop grabbed my hand and gave me a brilliant smile. "See? Nothing to worry about."

"Yeah," I replied, pretending I didn't notice the others hanging back and watching me. "Nothing to worry about."

We strolled down the street, drawing attention, the same mix of concerned and welcoming looks as before. The streets were packed and a lot of people greeted Bishop. He smiled, nodded, answered quick questions, and introduced me.

But the whole thing with almost everyone staring at me and talking to people I didn't know and didn't know that I could trust started to make me nervous again. It didn't matter how hard I tried to embrace those with welcoming smiles and friendly words, my insides were getting tighter and tighter.

As if able to read my mind, Bishop stopped introducing me and held my hand, letting me shyly hide in his shadow while he talked with people. I was sure it didn't make as good an impression as me trying to smile and returning people's greetings, but it felt a lot safer.

I'd never been in such a large group before and it was getting harder and harder to ignore all the things Merrick had drilled into me about no one wanting to see me or hear what I had to say. It made me furious and frustrated that I couldn't get him out of my head, but it was also a good reminder that I couldn't break my programming in a single day.

It was going to take time and I needed to remember to be kind to myself.

We made our way down the street, looking at booths and tents, drawing closer and closer to the actual market until we reached the playground beside the market where I'd sat at a picnic table a month ago watching kids running around and playing

Three of the picnic tables that had once been scattered around the greenspace had been pulled together creating one long table. It was covered with craft supplies, and half a dozen kids of various ages sat on the benches, working away on their projects, while Quinn sat at the end, talking with one of the older kids.

A few feet away, at another picnic table, sat a handful

of adults, half of them watching the kids and half chatting among themselves. Behind them, more kids enjoyed the playground, running and laughing, supervised by a few more adults, and to the side, under the shade of a big tree, was a baby and toddlers play area with a handful of teens and a few other adults taking care of the littlest ones.

It looked so idyllic, like I was in the middle of a movie. Everyone was happy and relaxed, and the kids were having a great time. And this time, watching normal children do normal children things, I didn't feel jealous and sad like I had the last time I'd been in the market. I was happy for them, happy that they were allowed to play and that they weren't afraid of the playground — which could have happened since the playground had been ground zero for the grimalkin attack.

The wind shifted and the amazing smells from the food vendors washed over me, making my stomach rumble, which made Bishop glance at me and laugh.

"I'd say that smells like lunch," he said just as Velora pushed through the crowd and rushed up to us. She flashed Bishop a saccharine smile that made my stomach churn, grabbed his free arm, and pushed her breasts against it.

"Otis and Rex are going at it again. Will you sweet talk them into behaving?" She fluttered her lashes and I was pretty sure she didn't mean the action in a sarcastic way. She actually thought it would attract Bishop and make him interested in her.

He sighed and glanced at me, a hint of frustration in his eyes that he kept from bleeding into his expression.

I forced a smile knowing everyone was watching, and at least a third of them, probably more like a half, were judging if I'd get in the way of pack business.

Velora sneered at me as if asking Bishop to do his job was a win for her and I struggled to keep my expression pleasant. If I got upset, I'd just be proving her and anyone who doubted me right. And I was *not* going to prove her right.

AUDREY

"Go," I told him as upbeat and happily as I could, making Velora's sneer falter. "It sounds important."

I dragged my gaze to the park, knowing I'd have to sit there alone until he returned, something that made me even more nervous, but then Quinn laughed at something, catching my attention, and I realized I didn't have to be alone. I could help Quinn with the kids while I waited, which would keep me busy with someone I trusted.

"I'll hang out with Quinn until you're done and then we'll have lunch," I added, not having to force myself to smile. So far, I'd enjoyed every moment I'd had with Quinn and something inside me assured me that I could trust her... and despite that something telling me I could also trust Cyrus, I was going to believe it.

Bishop glanced over my shoulder at Quinn's play station, his own smile deepening. "I won't be long."

Then he captured my lips in a quick but searing kiss that sent me reeling before he escorted me closer to the playground partitioned off for the kids.

"Hey, Audrey," Quinn called out. "Come to keep me company? My shift isn't done for another couple of hours."

I stepped off the street onto the park's soft grass and turned back to see Bishop still watching me and Velora tapping her foot impatiently while still smiling that too-sweet smile. I couldn't have been the only one to see through that smile, but no one was looking at her. They were all looking at me.

I stepped back, crossing the colorful barrier into the kids' space, and darkness flashed through Bishop's eyes as his wolf gave me a hungry look before he hurried away with Velora.

"I don't know what was hotter," Quinn whispered, fanning herself, "that kiss or that look."

I tried not to look at the crowd, who I knew were all still staring at me, as heat rushed over my face and down my neck. Both the kiss and the look were something better done in private and now the rumors wouldn't just be about me spending time with Bishop. They'd be about how Bishop had kissed me, which was juicier and would spread like wildfire through the festival.

"Come on," she said, saving me from spontaneously combusting from embarrassment. "Meet my pups for the day."

I approached the art station and all of the kids

instantly looked up at me, along with the adults at the nearby table.

I strengthened my smile and ignored the adults, hoping they wouldn't freak out that I was near their children. So far everyone who'd spoken to me had been nice. Everyone who looked wary or angry had just avoided me, but I was no longer with a pack alpha. Those who'd held their tongue before might not now.

"Everyone, this is Audrey," Quinn said, drawing my attention back to the kids.

The kids ranged from four or five to nine, maybe ten, and were a mix of boys and girls. Five of them greeted me, while the sixth, a little girl with big brown eyes and curly brown hair just stared at me.

She looked very familiar and I didn't get the impression that she was staring at me because she was curious about me. It was more like she was wary and not just wary about me but about everything. I understood how she was feeling even if I didn't know why.

I returned the kids' smiles and greetings while wracking my brain, trying to remember her. Then it hit me. She'd been a part of the group who I'd saved from the grimalkin, the girl who'd been sobbing. And beside her, hovering protectively close was the other girl, the one who'd been deathly pale and silent.

"Read us a story," the youngest kid of the group said, holding out a thin book in his gluey, paint-smeared hands.

"How about I tell you a story," I offered instead. I

would have loved to have read the book to them, but until I got some lessons, I wouldn't be reading anything to anyone.

"I want this story," the little guy insisted and the others voiced their agreement.

I smiled at his enthusiasm while trying to figure out a way to give them what they wanted. "It must be a great story."

The boy vigorously nodded and now I wanted to sit with them and read even more. Maybe even have them pile around me to help steady their shifter souls, especially the silent little girl because I knew about some of her trauma and ached to reassure her.

But I was a stranger. It wasn't my place to cuddle with them despite every instinct inside me screaming that I should.

"How about we finish our pieces of art first?" Quinn suggested, saving me from having to explain that I couldn't read. I wasn't sure if she'd figured that out or just thought I was reluctant to be around children.

But the kids all pouted. Even the two girls who I'd saved kept staring at me expectantly. They wanted my attention and I really wanted to give it to them, but I couldn't—

Except I could. I might not be able to read, but I could still spend time with them, and I had the perfect thing to entertain them.

I opened my satchel and pulled out the flipbook I was making to explain to Bishop how movies worked. It wasn't completely done, I wanted to draw a few more pictures to get the point across, but I was sure the kids wouldn't care.

"I think I have something just as good as a story." The little guy — still holding the book — scrunched up his face in disappointment. "I can make a picture dance."

I held up the roughly made book, catching everyone's attention. I hadn't asked for scissors and had had to rip the pages from my notebook then rip them into smaller pieces. The book hadn't been intended for anyone except Bishop, but again, I doubted the kids would care.

"Have you seen a flipbook before?" I asked them.

The kids shook their heads and they and Quinn gathered around me. The adults at the nearby bench stared at me, one with a wary expression the others curious.

Holding the edge of the book tight — since it was only held together by some string Eloise had given me — I flipped through the pages, making my stickman jump and turn and start to hop to the side.

The kids and Quinn gasped.

"Audrey, that's—" Quinn began.

"Again!" the little guy exclaimed, cutting her off, and the others picked up the call.

I flipped through the book two more times then scanned the picnic table, looking for paper. There was some, but not enough for all the kids to make their own book.

"Is it possible to get more paper?" I asked Quinn as I handed the book to the oldest kid and drew her aside. I wasn't far enough away for the kids not to hear me even if I whispered, but I was hoping the book would distract them since I didn't want to disappoint them if I couldn't get the paper.

"It's easy to make one of these," I continued, "and if the kids want, I can teach them to make one of their own."

Quinn sighed. "They'd love that, but I can't leave my post."

"I'll go," one of the adults, a woman in her mid-thirties, said as the others joined the kids to look at the book. "Gemma hasn't looked interested in anything since the grimalkin attack." She swallowed hard. "I didn't get a chance to thank you for saving my pups and here you are helping again."

"Her son and daughter were two of the kids you saved," Quinn said as she pointed to the silent little girl who still looked as closed off as before, with the exception that she was staring intently every time the older kid flipped the pages of my little book.

"Thank you, alpha," the woman said, running away before I could tell her not to call me that.

"Can you spread gossip?" I begged Quinn. "Please. People shouldn't call me that."

"Yes, they should. You're mated to Knox and from the way Bishop kissed you in front of everyone, it won't be long before you're mated with him, too."

"Still doesn't make me an alpha," I insisted.

"Kind of does," said the man who'd been looking at

me warily. His expression was still guarded, but it had softened a bit as if he was reconsidering how he felt about me — which I guessed was the whole reason I was here in public, letting everyone stare at me while I freaked out on the inside. "What is that thing?"

"It's a flipbook," I said and he raised his eyebrows telling me that wasn't a good enough explanation. "If you, ah... If you create a series of slightly different images going from one position to another and flip the pages at the right speed, it'll look like the image is moving."

"Fascinating." He turned back to the kids and watched as the older kid flipped the book again.

"Felix is an engineer," Quinn said. "Bishop mentioned that you might want to talk to one. He has to know how things work or it'll drive him crazy, so I'm sure he'll be able to help you. He belongs to Owen, the one you handed the book to."

"It's a pleasure to meet you." I nodded and respectfully shifted my gaze to his ear when he looked back at me, making him frown.

"Alpha, you show me too much respect," he replied, making me cringe.

"Please don't call me that. I'm just a girl who was fated for Knox." God, if calling me alpha caught on, Cyrus was going to kill me, and it wouldn't matter if I was mated to Knox.

"I have a feeling you're more than that. Beth says you're the one who nearly killed herself rescuing her kids."

"Well, I..." I had no idea how to respond to that. I couldn't have ignored them if I'd tried. It had been stupid and terrifying and I'd do it again if I had to.

"What were some of the things you wanted to talk to an engineer about?" Quinn asked, saving me from having to come up with a response.

I shot her a thankful look and she returned a warm smile before turning to the kids and herding them back to the art table.

"I've heard a rumor that you're from another realm," Felix said, pushing his hands in his pockets and watching his kid show one of the younger kids how to flip the book. "Is it true?"

"It is." And there were only two people who could have spread that rumor. Velora or Finn. Maybe that was why everyone was looking at me strangely. Except I knew it was mostly because I was mated to Knox, the strange, reclusive alpha of their pack... and *now* because Bishop had kissed me like he wanted me.

Felix nodded his head, his expression turning thoughtful. "That's why you want to talk with an engineer."

"And a scientist. I know about things that the pack might find useful, but I—" I dug my toe into the ground. Bishop had said sharing what I knew was a great idea, but everyone was going to be frustrated with me because I didn't know how anything worked. "I just know about them. I don't know how they work and for a lot of the things we'd need to figure out some kind of power source," I said, the words coming out in a rush, my heart in my throat, waiting for him to laugh at me.

"So you don't know how the flipbook works?"

"Oh, the flipbook is simple. The brain is great at filling in little blank spots. So when you draw the stickman moving in small increments then flip the pages, your brain fills in the action between one drawing and the next. It won't work if the movement between one drawing and the next is too big, but you don't need a million pictures with microscopic differences for it to work."

He frowned at me. "Microscopic?"

Right. Shit. They hadn't discovered microscopes yet. Whil had already told me that. There were some curved lenses in the realm for correcting vision, but the quality was rough and shifters didn't have bad eyesight so the pack hadn't explored that area of research.

"Microscopic means something that can only be seen by a microscope, which is a device with a lens or lenses, I'm not sure which, that helps you see small things that you couldn't normally see."

His frown deepened, but his eyes brightened as if he was fascinated with what I was saying. "Like what?"

I told him about viruses and things like pollen and mites and that there was a whole world of things we couldn't see that affect our bodies — or at least human bodies — and the water and the soil and the air we breathed.

I was in the middle of explaining telescopes when the

woman who'd run off to get the paper returned. Felix made me promise to meet with him again to hear more about the wonders of my realm and I sat at the table and taught the kids how to make their own flipbooks.

It didn't take long before the kids were hard at work creating their books, the youngest with Quinn's help and the sobbing girl I'd rescued from the grimalkins, Gemma, with her mother's.

The rest of the adults chatted amongst themselves, no longer worried about my presence, and with a sigh, I sat back, looked up at the perfect, cloudless sky, and let the kid's joyful chatter and the rush of conversation from those at the nearby booths wash over me. If I wasn't looking at the festival goers and seeing them stare at me, I could pretend I was part of all the excitement, that I belonged.

And maybe I did.

Maybe Bishop was right and his pack just needed to see me to realize how plain and ordinary I was. The kids hadn't cared that I was practically human or that I'd somehow mated their antisocial alpha, and once I'd gotten them excited about the flipbooks, their parents had stopped giving me serious looks. A few of them were still glancing over at me, but their expressions had changed to more curious than wary.

AUDREY

A FEW MINUTES LATER, AS THE NEW SMALL, HOPEFUL PEACE settled inside me, the boy closest to me, Holden, sat back and held up his flipbook, looking at me expectantly.

"What have you got?" I asked, crouching beside him.

He slowly flipped through the six pages that he'd drawn. He wasn't a very skilled artist — of course, he *was* seven so that could easily change — but his incremental position changes looked great.

"That's fantastic," I praised, making him puff out his chest. "A few more pages and you'll complete the action. What do you think your guy should do after he leaps over that rock?"

"Leap on it," he replied, his expression serious as if jumping onto the rock after jumping over it was the next logical action.

"Good idea. If you want to keep going after that, you

could make it look like he's running away from the rock or jumping up really high by drawing the rock farther and farther away from your guy—" I pointed at the space behind his stick figure and then a few more spots getting closer and closer to the spine of the book. "Or draw the rock getting smaller and smaller as your guy gets higher and higher."

My flipbook had been very simple, just a guy moving around, but this kid had already added a prop, and I hoped my little nudge helped him think about other ways he could work with the prop.

"Oh! I know!" he exclaimed and went back to drawing.

I straightened and let my gaze wander to the parents, praying I hadn't overstepped and that Holden's parent, whoever they were, wouldn't get upset with me.

But Felix gave me a nod of approval, making me wonder if Holden's parents had just dropped him off and hadn't stayed since Quinn hadn't indicated that Felix had more than one kid in the group.

And now that I thought about it, it was kind of surprising to see so many adults standing around watching. I'd gotten the impression this area was a form of daycare and that they weren't required to help out.

"They were about to leave when you showed up with the flipbook," Quinn chuckled as if she could read my mind, although my wondering was probably obvious in my expression. "You know she doesn't bite," she added to the others.

One of the women offered an embarrassed smile. "We didn't—"

"You're mated to Knox and—" the man beside her said.

Felix huffed. "She's obviously not like Knox. She's here talking to us, showing our pups something new and exciting."

"But Knox has to be watching," the man protested. "He flattened a third of Stonehaven just to get to her. I don't want to risk saying something wrong and have him go after me."

"He's not going to go after you," Quinn said, glancing at the kids who thankfully weren't paying attention to the conversation. "He's never seriously hurt a pack member."

"He would for his mate," the first woman said.

"Then don't threaten her," Quinn shot back as if it was obvious.

"But we don't know anything about her," the first woman said, making me cringe. It looked like I hadn't done enough to ease their worries.

"Then talk to her." Quinn threw her hands up in exasperation.

Do you need me to rescue you? Knox asked.

My gaze jumped straight to a shadow in the grasses between a red tent and a booth with yellow and green triangle flags.

Knox.

I knew without a doubt that it wasn't a grimalkin like it had been a month ago when I'd been in the same playground watching happy families being happy. It was my mate.

A hint of worry seeped through our bond and I could tell Knox was willing to leave the safety of the shadows to rescue me. He didn't want to, but he'd do it.

I shook my head and tried to calm myself. They were just talking. Felix and Gemma's mother had relaxed around me, the others would, too. Eventually.

Except it was the eventually part and how long that would take that concerned me. Which set off my worry and desire to shrink in on myself and become less noticeable.

"Excuse me," I murmured, needing to get away from them to refocus on what worries were real and what was the product of my upbringing. "I should find a table for lunch."

I clasped my hands in front of me to stop them from trembling and strolled away from the craft table while everything inside me screamed to hurry up, be invisible, just for a moment.

Are you sure? Knox growled. *You just say the word.*

I nodded yes. Then realized Knox might think that was me asking him to rescue me, so I shook my head, then huffed realizing that wasn't clear, either.

I pushed some love through our bond, trying to will him to understand that I just needed a moment and that I could stay strong until Bishop came back because his plan for his pack to see me *was* making them more welcoming.

I've finally managed to get rid of Velora and clear up the non-argument. Getting food now, Bishop said in my head.

About time, Knox huffed. *She's uncomfortable being alone.*

I left her with Quinn, Bishop protested.

And Quinn is only one person and she's responsible for looking after the pups, not Audrey.

I opened my mouth to tell them it was fine then snapped it shut. There was no point in saying anything. I was too far away from both of them to be heard and speaking into the air would only make people more wary of me.

I'd never wanted telepathic communication more than I did now, even if it was just to tell them to shut up. But I couldn't, so I just had to put up with them arguing in my head.

Straining to ignore them, I let my gaze wander to a nearby game street at the side of the park with booths that had all manner of games. There weren't as many people down the impromptu street as there'd been on the other narrow streets through the festival, but that only meant it wasn't crowded. Families played games and cheered each other on, a large group of eager-looking kids gathered around a booth with bright blue stripes, and—

A hint of gold caught in sunlight flashed for a second and I turned my attention back to the group of kids to see Cyrus stand up. He must have been hunched over or crouching in the middle of the group for me not to have seen him when I first looked because he stood easily a head taller than most of the kids.

He said something and ruffled the hair of one of the kids, making the young man beam with pride, then he turned to someone else. The kids hung onto every word he said, but I didn't get the impression it was because he was commanding them. No, they all looked excited and happy.

"So what's the plan?" Cyrus asked, making me realize I'd wandered close enough to hear him.

My heart stuttered, but I couldn't make myself walk away so I turned to face the playground, praying it wasn't obvious that I was eavesdropping.

God, it was the stupidest thing I could have done. He'd already told me to remember my place and accused me of sneaking around, but my body had frozen on the spot. In fact, something inside me was screaming that I needed to get closer.

I'd never seen Cyrus look so relaxed, so comfortable, and the kids looked at him with adoration. They clearly loved him and weren't afraid of him.

So, it's just me he hates.

But that thought didn't feel right, no matter how scared I was of him. What I saw now was a kinder softer version of the gruff man who I'd walked with for a month. The man who I'd originally thought he was.

Except that didn't fit with the man who'd yelled at me and it was always safer to assume someone was more dangerous than they might be.

"Meet your little brother or sister," a young man said, his voice cracking. "Buy them lunch and play games."

"And win a toy for them," another guy said, this one a few years younger than the first.

"And don't mention the attack," added one of the girls, making me look back at the group.

"Right," Cyrus said. "We want them to forget for a day who they've lost or who's still in the hospital."

All the kids nodded and Cyrus handed out coin purses.

I couldn't stop staring. It sounded like Cyrus had arranged for a group of older kids to help younger kids have fun at the festival, kids who'd suffered during the grimalkin attack.

That certainly wasn't the man who'd yelled at me or who said veiled threats about ruining my dinner or being on time.

My fantasy rushed through my mind's eye. He was always gentle and loving. He always held me with such tenderness and looked at me like I was the most precious thing in the world as he pushed inside me to ease the heat fever from burning me up.

For a second, it felt like it was more than just a fantasy, like the moment between us had been real.

But that was the Cyrus I wanted him to be, the Cyrus he was showing to these kids and the rest of their pack. Not the Cyrus he was with me.

The thought made my throat tighten and the fantasy slipped away.

"Don't forget to have fun yourselves," he said as they all rushed past me into the park to a group of young kids waiting on the other side.

Oh, shit.

I froze, holding my breath as if that would make me invisible even though I was standing out in the open. I didn't want to find out how he'd react to me listening in and could only pray he wouldn't want to make a scene in front of his pack.

Worry swelled through our mating bond and I pushed as much love back at Knox as I could, hoping to reassure him. I didn't want him upset enough that he'd run into the middle of the festival. That could only spell disaster.

Out of the corner of my eye, I watched Cyrus head deeper down the makeshift street and released the breath I'd been holding, relief flooding me... as well as disappointment. I didn't want to be invisible to him or ignored by him. I wanted the Cyrus of my fantasies.

But that was never going to happen.

AUDREY

"Hey, gorgeous," Bishop said a moment later from somewhere behind me.

I turned around, my heart skipping a beat with joy as I saw him *and* the heated look in his eyes.

"Hey," I replied, suddenly feeling shy, my cheeks warming.

He held up two paper bags in one hand and a large paper cup in the other. "I've got lunch. Have you found us a place to sit?"

"Sit with me," Quinn said from a nearby bench. "I've got twenty minutes and wouldn't mind the company."

"Do you need lunch?" I asked as we sat beside her. "We can get you something if you can't leave."

"Nope," she said and jerked her thumb toward the park's entrance just as Zavier hurried inside. "All taken care of."

"But I can't stay," Zavier said, rushing over to us. "My

shift starts in two minutes and I need to be on the other side of the festival."

"Then what are you waiting for?" Quinn laughed, taking the bag and making a shooing motion.

Zavier huffed and she flashed him a brilliant smile, making him huff again before taking off.

"Thank you. You're the best!" she called after him and I couldn't help but wonder just what their relationship was.

Bishop pulled a sandwich out of one of our bags and handed it to me, while Quinn carefully pulled out a steaming meat pie.

"Sisters, I love these pies," Quinn sighed, staring at her food. "But they're only ever made during the summer festival."

"So, ah..." Did I dare ask? It was kind of a personal question. "That was awfully nice of Zavier to bring you one," I said instead.

"Yeah, he's the best." She glanced at me and raised an eyebrow. "And whatever you're thinking, it's wrong."

"How do you know what I was thinking?" I asked, making Bishop chuckle.

"Kind of obvious because it's what all of us have been thinking for years," he said.

"He's practically my brother," she shot back.

"But not." Bishop waggled his eyebrows at me and flashed me a wicked smile. "Zavier's family took in Quinn when her parents were killed. You guys were what? Five or six?"

"Seven," Quinn corrected, "and, no. I don't care what everyone has been saying for the last five years. He's my brother."

"But you're so good together," Bishop pressed.

"Because we're family." She pinched the bridge of her nose. "He's a watchman because his father, his uncle, his grandfather, and who-knows-how-many other relatives are. It's what's expected of him, but I know he'd rather become a hunter or a merchant or anything that will get him out of this town." Her expression turned wistful, but I couldn't tell if it was because she wanted to join him or if she was in love with him and knew she couldn't be what he needed. "I'm happy here with my kids. I'll help Zavier make his dream come true and I'll find a nice guy or—" she winked at me "—a couple of guys to settle down with to have my own pups."

I took a bite of my sandwich, a creation loaded with chicken — or the equivalent of it in this realm — a few grilled vegetables, and a delicious spread that tasted like a spicy mayonnaise, hoping it wasn't obvious to Quinn how I felt. I could see why everyone thought they'd mate. Even from the first moment I'd seen them, I could tell they were close and they both seemed to look at each other with something more than brotherly or sisterly affection. Of course, I doubt either could see that, and if Quinn was so sure that they wanted different things then nothing would happen between them.

"So, the pups really liked your flipbook," Quinn said, not even trying to hide her change of conversation. "I have a feeling we're going to be making them for the rest of the festival."

"A flipbook?" Bishop asked.

"Show him," Quinn insisted, holding out my flipbook to me.

I set my sandwich back in its bag, took the book, and flipped the pages. "I was making it for you to explain how movies work."

"That's amazing." He took the book from me and flipped the pages. "And you said the pups are making them?"

"Audrey showed them how." Quinn nudged me with her elbow. "You know if you haven't figured out what you want to do with yourself, you should consider becoming a teacher. You were so patient with the kids and they loved you."

"I, ah..." It was a kind offer and a part of me loved the idea, but another part was afraid of angry parents. Sure the parents at the craft tables had warmed up to me but not everyone would and I doubted they wanted someone like me spending all day with their children. Half an hour in the park, sure, but not a whole day at school.

"No need to decide now. Just wanted to suggest it." Quinn finished her pie, stood, and brushed the remaining crumbs from her dress. "Are you going to the dance later?"

"Of course we are," Bishop said.

"Then I'll see you there." She hurried back to the craft

tables and was met with bright smiles and cheerful hellos from the children.

"Almost done?" Bishop asked me as I took my second to last bite of my sandwich.

I nodded and his smile deepened.

"Good, because there's so much more I want to show you."

For the rest of the afternoon, we strolled through the festival's winding streets, looking at all the amazing things for sale, eating far too many treats, and playing all the games.

At the beginning, I was still far too aware of everyone staring at me, but as the day wore on and people stopped asking Bishop who I was, I stopped noticing their stares. I was having too much fun with Bishop, laughing at his bad jokes, cheering him on when he tried to win me prizes, and overall feeling amazing.

I'd never felt so happy and by the time we'd made our way to a big square lit with fairy lights and lanterns, my cheeks were sore from smiling so much.

The square was filled with people dancing, others watching the dancing, and those just standing around chatting.

"Dance with me," Bishop said, tugging me closer to the dancers.

They were gathered in paired lines and were stepping and spinning and hopping in a crazy pattern that everyone seemed to know.

I slowed down, pulling back from the group. "I don't know the steps."

"It doesn't matter. Look." He pointed to a preteen who obviously didn't know all the steps but everyone around him didn't seem to care. They were all laughing and having a good time.

Alright, maybe I could join in. And really, after its initial rocky start, I was having a great day. So great, I didn't want it to end. "Okay."

Bishop flashed me a heart-stopping smile and drew me to the edge of the bystanders. Beyond the dancers, on the far side of the square, were the musicians on a raised platform. They were a mix of hand drum, some kind of flute, and two stringed instruments that looked like guitars but had more twang, and they laughed and sang while they played. The music was upbeat and folky and the drum was like a steady heartbeat urging me to move within seconds of listening.

A moment later, the song came to an end and Bishop led me to the back of a line beside an elderly couple who'd been moving just as sprightly as everyone else.

"Alpha!" the woman joyfully exclaimed, shifting to make more room for us. "I was wondering why you weren't playing tonight."

"You play an instrument?" I asked.

The man chuckled. "He plays *all* the instruments."

"But not at the same time," the woman added, making the man laugh louder.

"No," the man replied, "but that would be something to see. I'm Guthrie and this is my mate Embry."

"Audrey," I replied, my insides tightening as the conversation moved from Bishop to me.

"Are you enjoying your first festival?" Embry asked with no sign of wariness or disgust in her expression.

"I am," I told her, still a little hesitant.

The band played the first few cords of the next song telling the dancers to get ready. Bishop held both my hands, the look of happiness and love in his eyes making my shifter connection to him warm even more, and then we were hopping and spinning and laughing.

AUDREY

WE DANCED TO FOUR SONGS BEFORE THE CROWD CAJOLED Bishop into playing, but I didn't mind. The last song had been the fastest yet, and I was completely out of breath so I hung out with Quinn while she waited for Zavier to finish his shift and Bishop stepped onto the stage.

He picked up one of the twangy guitars, sat on a nearby stool, and strummed a few notes.

Beside me, Quinn sighed and her expression softened. "I love this song."

Other women had the same reaction while a few people — including Guthrie and Embry — glanced my way with soft smiles.

Then Bishop slowly played the first four melancholy bars, drew in a breath, and started to sing, his gaze locked on me.

The song was sweet and sad and hopeful, about a

man longing for his fated mate, knowing she was out there but never having met her.

I could see why Quinn loved it and Bishop had an amazing, emotive voice that seemed to reach out to me and warm our shifter connection even though he was on the other side of the dance floor. And the way he wouldn't stop looking at me, with yearning and love in his eyes deepened the feeling.

I ached and yearned along with him and the song, and I knew in my heart that Knox *and* Bishop were the men I'd waited my whole life to find. They were my fate... and so, according to the aching in my soul, was Cyrus.

The song concluded with the final few bars turning happy and the man finding his fated mate. Bishop held my gaze as the final notes faded, looking at me like I was the only woman in the world.

Quinn sighed, caught in the musical spell Bishop had woven, and I had to agree with her. That was the most beautiful thing I'd ever heard.

"Wow," Quinn breathed. "When Bishop wants to make a statement, he really makes a statement. He just made his intentions about you clear to everyone here."

I glanced around nervously, but while there were some women glaring daggers at me, everyone else was either happy or didn't seem to care that Bishop had basically said I was the one he'd been searching for even though I was also Knox's mate.

Then someone started clapping, breaking the silence, and everyone else joined in, clapping and cheering. The

rest of the band, who'd let him have his solo perfor-
mance, nodded their approval, while the drummer
flashed him a knowing smile.

Bishop gave me another heated look then turned his
attention back to the crowd as he strummed a few upbeat
chords making all the dancers scramble to get into
position.

"Dance with me!" Quinn exclaimed, and she grabbed
my hand and pulled me to the end of one of the dance
rows.

She easily stepped into the next move without
missing a beat despite the dancing having already started
and laughed good-naturedly at me as I stumbled to catch
up. I laughed with her and continued to stumble through
the rest of the dance like I had with all the other dances
before.

After Bishop's third song, he bowed to his audience,
handed the guitar back to its owner, and pushed through
the crowd heading straight for me.

Heat burned my cheeks but I was determined to push
through my embarrassment. He'd sung me a love song.
No one had ever sung me a love song before, and I was
filled with awe and joy.

"That first song was beautiful," I said as he picked me
up and spun us around.

"A beautiful song for a beautiful woman." He cupped
my cheeks, his eyes shining with affection, and pressed a
breathtaking kiss against my lips, leaving me reeling and
overflowing with joyful emotions.

For just a moment, I didn't care that people were looking at me and wondering who the hell I was to have the eye of the pack's most eligible bachelor. All I could see was the desire in Bishop's eyes and feel the heat of our connection growing stronger the longer he kissed me.

After that, we talked and laughed and danced and ate treats deep into the night until I was so tired, I could barely keep my eyes open.

"I think it's time to go home," he said as I sleepily clung to him, my head resting against his arm and my heart overflowing.

"One more dance?" I begged.

I was going to be so sore in the morning but I didn't care. I was having more fun than I'd ever had in my life and didn't want tomorrow morning to shatter the magical spell Bishop had cast over me. It was like I was Cinderella and I wanted to stop time so the clock never struck twelve.

"Your mate is waiting to give you a private dance in the summer garden," he replied, his voice deepening and sending heat rushing through me.

The memory of how Knox and I had *danced* last night in Whil's greenhouse heated my insides and now I was torn. Being with Knox and connecting with him had felt amazing and I wanted to do it again, but I didn't want to leave Bishop, didn't want this amazing day to end... of course maybe he could stay with me and Knox.

He had mentioned the possibility of being with both

of them at the same time back in Kelna and the thought had turned me on.

It had also embarrassed the hell out of me, but that hadn't stopped me from thinking about it.

I hugged him tighter and opened my mouth to invite him to join me and Knox, but I couldn't make myself say it.

Blazing heat radiated from my face and I was grateful for the dim light. I was also frustrated that talking about sex still embarrassed me, but I had to remind myself that I was taking baby steps. I'd had sex with both of them and was no longer embarrassed that they'd seen me naked. Eventually I'd work up to talking about it or even asking for what I wanted.

Bishop frowned at me. He'd noticed that I'd been about to say something and then cut myself off, so I smiled at him, showing him just how happy I felt and how grateful I was that he'd given me this amazing day.

"I had a great time today," I said.

"Me, too." He led us away from the square packed with people and up the wide main road.

Ahead of us, the Residence stood tall and proud at the top of the rise, standing sentinel over the town, lit by the realm's two moons, and looking like a fairy tale. Just like how my whole day had felt.

The last upbeat song I'd heard jumped into my head and I skipped beside him, humming the tune, despite being sleepy. It was a really catchy tune and I was sure I was going to be singing it for the rest of the week, a thought that made my smile deepen.

The song was going to remind me all week of the amazing day I'd had and the hope that I'd have more amazing days with Bishop and Knox.

Then Bishop started to actually sing the song — I hadn't realized it had words — and with a whoop of joy I danced ahead of him, hopping and whirling and laughing.

With another whoop, I spun around to face him to see his eyes light up, his expression mirroring the happiness inside me. Behind him, the festival's lights lit the market, and even halfway up the road, I could hear bits of music and cheering and the roar of many voices talking. It was the most beautiful, most amazing thing I'd ever seen and I wanted to remember it forever. I didn't know how my life had gone from beaten down and despised to this, but I wasn't going to question it.

For once, something was going my way and it felt good, incredibly, amazingly good.

"You liked that song?" He sang a few more bars and I beamed at him.

"It's catchy and my last one of the night." I spun another full circle and held out my hands to him. "But I really liked the one you sang to me."

I spun again, and when I stopped, he was suddenly close, his eyes dark, the flecks of green so bright they looked like they glowed.

"I meant what I sang," he said, cupping my cheek with his palm.

I leaned into his touch, breathed in his fresh-cut grass scent, and sank deeper into his mesmerizing gaze.

"You're the one I've been searching for and I want everyone to know that I'm yours."

My smile turned wry. "Pretty sure everyone will know by the end of the night."

He'd made no attempt to hide how he felt about me all day and singing that song while never looking away from me had confirmed whatever gossip he'd started this afternoon.

And while I knew I'd made some female enemies today, right now, with my heart so full I thought it would burst, I didn't care. Bishop only had eyes for me and I felt like I was in an amazing dream.

"Then my plan was a success." He brushed his lips against mine.

It was just a whisper of a kiss, but it sent tingles racing down my spine, warming my heart and heating my core.

"I wanted everyone to know how I feel about you. If I hadn't made it obvious by singing *Fated Stars* then I'll scream it from the Residence's highest tower."

His words sparked within me and my soul soared with joy. This was right. This was the way it was supposed to be. Love. Happiness. Home.

He captured my lips in a powerful, hungry kiss. Hot slick heat raced through me, pooling low within me, and I moaned into his mouth. He took advantage of my parting lips and raked his tongue against mine, fueling my desire.

He was an incredible man, so full of joy and so accepting. Not once had he made me feel small or pathetic. Everything he'd done had been to show me that I deserved a place at his side, that I was worthy and special and wanted.

I was so in love with Bishop, I thought my heart would burst.

"You're my mate, Audrey," he growled against my lips, his wolf rising to the surface. "I love you."

AUDREY

I STARED INTO HIS WOLF-DARKENED EYES, FALLING INTO
their bottomless depths surrounded by brilliant green
stars and my heart soared at his words. He loved me.

He. Loved. Me.

No one had ever said those words to me and I knew
deep in my soul that Bishop was mine just as much as
Knox was.

"I love you—"

But Bishop's grip tightened, his body suddenly tense,
and he shoved me to the side, hard.

I stumbled, lost my balance, and fell onto my butt as
someone dressed head to toe in thick black clothing, his
face hidden by a heavy hood, plunged the claws on both
of his hands into Bishop's chest.

Oh, God! My heart leaped into my throat and I scrambled to my feet.

Bishop roared, the sound a mix of pain and rage,

pushed his hands up between the man's arms, and shoved his claws away. The action made the man's arms fly wide, and Bishop tore the claws of his right hand through the man's side with a spray of unnaturally bright red blood.

The man screeched. The sound was barely human, sending fear racing down my spine and chilling my blood, and for a second, I feared this man wasn't another shifter, he was something else, something dangerous.

But that didn't make sense. Underneath his bulky clothes, he was shaped like a man, and his claws, while hard to see in the dim light, looked like shifter's claws.

Bishop swiped his other hand at the man but he twisted out of the way to avoid Bishop's attack and dragged both sets of his claws through Bishop's side.

More blood splattered on the road by Bishop's feet and oozed between his fingers as the man jerked his attention to me.

Time stuttered to a halt, my pulse slow, dragging thuds, crushing around my heart. With the hood pulled low and the dim illumination from the streetlight, I couldn't see his face — all I could see were shadows — but his body language was threatening and I knew, without a doubt, that he wanted me dead.

I backed up a step, everything within me screaming to run. Run Now!

I couldn't help Bishop fight. I didn't know how to fight and I was slower than Bishop which meant I was slower than the man. I was better off screaming at the top of my lungs and finding help.

Except I knew the second I looked away, the man would jump on me.

With another screech, time lurched back to its regular speed, and the man surged forward. I scrambled back and slammed my back against the closest building, missing the alley behind me by three feet.

Oh shit oh shit oh shit.

The man raised his hands, ready to tear me open with his claws when Bishop snagged the back of his thick, oversized shirt and yanked. His claws grazed the front of my shirt, tearing the fabric but missing my flesh and before I could blink, the man had turned and rammed Bishop with his shoulder.

They both fell to the ground, the man on top, one set of claws already digging into Bishop's chest, the other about to slash open Bishop's throat.

"No!" I screamed, the sound tearing out of me, bringing the bitter acidic bite of bile rolling up my throat while sudden violent nausea erupted in my stomach.

The man froze, his attention snapping to me, and my stomach heaved as more bile burned my throat.

No no no.

Bishop raked his claws at the man's chest, but somehow the man noticed even though he was still staring at me and leaped up and out of the way. His body shuddered and Bishop lunged for him again, fast enough to tear into his calf with another spray of too-bright blood.

More bile burned up my throat and my stomach heaved.

Another shudder swept through the man's body as he dodged Bishop's next swipe and then he raced into the closest alley.

With a growl, Bishop scrambled to his feet to chase after him but staggered and dropped to one knee after only a few steps.

I rushed to his side as he sagged to the ground, trying to swallow back the bile and not throw up. Blood soaked his clothes, a mix of his and the assailant's, although the brightness in the man's blood was quickly fading and was now almost indistinguishable from Bishop's.

"Do you need a med pack?" I asked, trying to get a look at how deep the man had dug into his chest. "Where's the closest one?"

During the first aid class, Nova had mentioned where the packs were, but I didn't know any of the street names or the city's layout and had planned to ask her about it the next time I saw her.

"There's one—" He groaned and clutched his chest, making my panic spike.

Oh, God. Were his injuries so bad he actually needed an elixir?

"Can you shift?" *Please say you can shift.* Even if the shift didn't fully heal his injuries, it would still help. Except if the injury was severe enough, he wouldn't have enough strength to complete the transformation and it could kill him.

He groaned and shook his head, making my pulse spike. I had to get a vial of the healing elixir into him. Now.

"Where? Where is it?" I grabbed his arm, helping to steady him, and he raised his gaze to meet mine.

"It's—" He sucked in a sharp, sudden breath and his eyes widened.

Fear and agony raced through his expression as strange black and red veins bulged under his skin and raced up his neck.

A strangled cry fell from his lips and he locked eyes with me, making my pulse stall completely.

"Love you," he gasped. "I—"

With another cry, he lurched back onto the road and started convulsing.

Oh no. Oh no no no.

This couldn't be happening. Not now. Not after he'd told me that he loved me. Today was supposed to have been happy and wonderful. I'd been overflowing with joy a moment ago and now... now I couldn't catch my breath.

Something was horribly wrong with Bishop, more than just being beaten up in a fight, and it had everything to do with that man. The strange black and red veins meant he'd cast a spell or cursed him or... poisoned him.

That was the most logical explanation, more logical than magic even though magic was more prevalent in this realm than the mortal realm. That man had to have poisoned Bishop because if it was anything else there might not be a cure.

My breath caught in my too-tight throat. It *was* poison and there *was* an antidote. There had to be.

"Help!" I screamed, scrambling to get his head onto my lap to protect it from the stone road. I didn't know where the med pack was, I couldn't contact anyone telepathically, and I couldn't leave him to get help, not without him bashing his head on the ground.

God, no. Please. I couldn't be useless like Merrick and Sterling had said I was my entire life. I just couldn't be.

"Please," I sobbed.

Bishop was dying. It was obvious from the pallor of his skin and the way his body convulsed as the veins grew thicker, now covering his cheeks and forearms.

It had happened so fast, the attack, the poison. Everything... and just after he'd told me that he loved me, told his whole pack, really. He hadn't been embarrassed of me for being so weak I couldn't shift. He'd sung me a love song and kissed me in public and... God!

I bit back another sob and ground my teeth together.

I. Was. Not. Useless.

That was Sterling and Merrick's poison. Not the truth.

I'd killed a grimalkin. It might have been by accident, but I killed one, and I sure as hell could save Bishop. If I couldn't get help to come to me, I'd go to the help.

I grabbed Bishop under the shoulders and heaved. He was as heavy as I'd thought he'd be, which was heavier than I could realistically manage with him writhing in agony, but I *was not* going to let him die.

He convulsed again, jerking out of my grip and bashing his head against my foot. Pain shot through my toes, making me cry out, but I didn't stop. I couldn't stop. I had to save him.

I grabbed him again and dragged him farther down the street as fast as I could, my hands hurting with how tightly I gripped his shirt. It wasn't far. I could make it and I wouldn't let go again. I wouldn't let go, ever. Just a little farther and someone would hear me.

Please, God.

"Help!"

Don't miss the next book in the series!

Wolf Decided

Ensnared by the Pack: Book Five

OTHER BOOKS BY TESSA COLE

NEPHILIM'S DESTINY

Destined Shadows, prequel story

Destined Darkness, book 1

Destined Blood, book 2

Destined Fire, book 3

Destined Storm, book 4

Destined Radiance, book 5

ANGEL'S FATE

Fated Bonds, book 1

Fated Winter, book 2

Fated Fear, book 3

Fated Despair, book 4

Fated Resolve, book 5

Fated Heart, book 6

THE GRECIAN GODDESS TRILOGY

Kiss of the Goddess, book 1

Power of the Goddess, book 2

Bonds of the Goddess, book 3

ENSNARED BY THE PACK

www.ingramcontent.com/pod-product-compliance
Lightning Source LLC
Chambersburg PA
CBHW030116180626
46812CB00002B/434

* 9 7 8 1 9 9 0 5 8 7 2 0 7 *